TEARS OF A GANGSTER

TERRANT(HOP) HAMILTON

authorHOUSE®

AuthorHouse™
1663 Liberty Drive
Bloomington, IN 47403
www.authorhouse.com
Phone: 1 (800) 839-8640

Published by AuthorHouse 07/11/2019

ISBN: 978-1-7283-1896-7 (sc)
ISBN: 978-1-7283-1895-0 (e)

Library of Congress Control Number: 2019909555

Let's go back, way back to June of 2000. Terry Hampton, a local small time drug dealer better known as T-Money was just trying to come up in a dog eat dog world. After struggling so much early in life T-Money knew that the time was now or never to make a serious change in life. Even though he had just graduated to a nine to five, he knew this was not going to accommodate the life he wanted to live.

While he was sitting there thinking of how he was going to come up his main man, Strapp, was doing the same thing. Now Strapp was the exact opposite of T-Money in many ways. For starters, Strapp stood about six feet or six feet and one inch tall on a good day. He was light skinned with wavy hair and weighed about two hundred and fifteen pounds. T-Money on the other hand was six feet and three inches tall; brown skinned and weighed about two hundred and thirty pounds. Both had bad tempers but where Strapp would just react, T-Money was more of a thinker. Together they were a force not many would dare to cross. As you can imagine Strapp, whose real name is Tony Bean, got his nickname because he always had his guns on him… two nine millimeters that his uncle gave him. T-Money got his nickname because he was always on the grind for his paper and the T was short for Terry. He also liked to keep his guns on him (two Desert Eagle forty-fives) because he always said it was better to be caught with them than to get caught slipping without them!

"Hey Strapp, it's time for us to start making some serious money, dawg, so we can get our peeps out the hood and live like kings. You feel me?"

"Yeah. I was just sitting here thinking the same thing but since you always be planning shit I know you would be coming up with a game plan."

"Well check this out. One of the Jamaican hoes I fuck with said she could get her uncle to put us down."

"Word?"

"Yeah. So I don't even have to ask you if you down because I respect your gangsta and if I got then you got."

"And you know I feel the same way so when we gonna get it popping?"

"As soon as I catch up with the hoe Slim T."

"Oh that's the girl you talking about."

"Yeah. What's up, you know her people?"

"Not personally but I heard they strong like a motherfucka! I ain't know you was hitting that."

"Yeah I been digging her back out for about a month."

"Damn! And she already wants to put you down?"

"You know how I do."

"Yeah, you must have hit her with some of that golden head. Ha, ha, ha."

"Of course I did but its two things you forgetting. One is licking that pussy is always the shit but if you ain't laying the pipe right then you wasting time. And second of all, don't get it twisted them other niggas' head might be gold but my shit is platinum." The both of them laughed so hard until they were crying.

As they were walking, Strapp noticed a little scuffle on the side road.

"Hey man, ain't that the chick Slim T car right there?"

"Sure is. What the fuck is going on?"

"I don't know but let's check this shit out."

"So you fucking the little nigga T-Money and you ain't got time for me no more you little bitch." Slap, Slap.

"Stop. Stop, Ricky."

"Nah, and ain't no use to worry about telling your peeps because I'm going to kill your hot little ass!"

"Damn my nigga, you talking some big boy shit hitting on a woman and all."

"This shit ain't none of your B.I. (business) so you better step the fuck off before…."

"Before what big boy?" Strapp asked as he stepped around the corner with his two toys in hand.

"Look man, y'all can have the little bitch just let me go on my way."

"Oh so now you want to leave but just a minute ago you was talking big shit!"

"I tell you what Slim T, why don't you head on home and I'll call you in a little bit."

"Are you sure Money?"

"Does shit stink?"

"Okay, I'll be waiting for your call." As Slim T was leaving, she got a funny feeling in the pit of her stomach. It wasn't because of nothing she ate. It was the look in T-Money's eyes that had her stomach turning flips. And then on top of that he had his crazy, ride or die, best friend with him, Strapp. She had heard stories of the two and what kind of damage they could do. After seeing that look in T-Money's eyes and seeing Strapp standing there with those two guns in his hand, she knew Ricky would not escape death.

"Look man, I got about 50 g's in the car. Just take it and let me live. I'll leave town and you'll never hear from me again and the girls is all yours."

"Nigga, shut up! You think this is about some pussy? You softer than you look. Let me educate your dumb ass. First of all, it's never personal. It's always business. When her peeps find out that I saved her life from some pussy-whipped bitch ass nigga like you they'll be grateful for life. And seeing as how they got all the dope I guess I won't be on the corner hustling anymore. So in your next life stop thinking with the little head and let the big head get some action." And those were the last words spoken before Strapp emptied two whole clips in his body.

"Hey man, you want to leave this nigga right here?"

"Hell yeah. Ain't nobody see us so fuck 'em."

"Word, then let's be out."

"Say Money?"

"What's up Strapp?"

"When did you come up with all that shit you told that nigga?"

"While he was begging like some kind of pussy!"

"See that's the shit I'm talking about. You be on some Matlock shit all the time."

"In the game we play, you always need a game plan. But more important you got to be a quick thinker. Now fuck the small talk, let's go get paid!"

Ring, ring, ring. "Hello."
"What's up baby girl?"
"Oh hey, T-Money. I was getting worried."
"No need to worry, Ma. I got you."
"Well, my uncle wants you to come by."
"Oh word!"
"Yeah, I told him what went down and he told me to tell you to come by."
"Check it, we gonna stop by the store and we'll be right there."
"Okay, I'll see you when you get here."
"Alright, peace out."
"Damn, my nigga. Why you didn't tell her you love her?"
"Shitttttt! The only things I love is moms and money."
"What about me?"
"Shit, that's not even a question. What a nigga want to do to you, he got to do to me first and that's real."
"That's the shit my nigga because you know I'll kill a whole army for you and Mrs. Hampton or die trying."
"That's why we boys till the end and fuck the bullshit."

As they pulled in front of Slim T's house, T-Money ran it to his boy how it might go down.
"Check this Strapp."
"What's up, Money?"
"When we get in here don't feel disrespected if he talks directly to me."
"Nah playa, I'm with you. He ain't got to never say shit to me, ever. Just as long as he knows I got ya back at all costs and that's word to my mother."
"It shouldn't be that type of party but it is you know we'll light this bitch up like the 4th of July." And with that being said they both got out.

Ding dong, ding dong. "Come on in."
"What's up Slim T?"
"Ain't nothing, boo. My uncle is in the back room. Go on back."
"Hey Slim T, I'm gonna chill out here with you." Said Strapp.
"Okay, that's cool. You want something to eat?"
"Nah, I'm cool but bring me a soda if you got one."
"Alright, make yourself at home."

Knock, knock, knock. "Come on in. It's T-Money right?"
"Yeah or Just Money for short."
"Well, my name is Uncle Sha and first of all let me just say I'm truly thankful for what you done for Tiesa."
"Who?"

"Oh, I forgot y'all call her Slim T."

"Yeah, I know her real name but since we don't use it, it kind of caught me off guard."

"But that's good, in the life we live names can sometimes be dangerous and deadly. Now before we go any further with this conversation, I want you to know that I could pay you for what you did today and that would be enough money that you could leave the game alone."

"I tell you what, Uncle Sha, let's just say you owe me one. I know the worth of your niece's life is priceless but if I take that money then that would make our relationship personal. And with me nothing's ever personal, it's always business!"

"And why is that?"

"Because when things are personal they can affect your business decisions and we both know a bad decision in the game is the difference between prison and freedom or more important, life or death!"

After several hours of talking everything was set up. T-Money would receive 50 kilos a month with the first package to be delivered by the end of the week. Because of the liking that Uncle Sha took to T-Money he told him that he would never have to worry about transporting the drugs or money because everything would be arranged. He also told him that when the package arrived his three nephews would also arrive and would be thee to handle any kind of problem that might come about. When T-Money said it would just be him and his boy, Strapp, Uncle Sha simply told him that this wasn't personal it was strictly business and that they should get to know each other. With that being said the conversation was ended.

After T-Money and Strapp left Uncle Sha called Tiesa in the room. "Well Uncle Sha what do you think of him?"

"I think he's a good kid trying to make the right moves. How do you feel about him?"

"I really like him but I don't know how he feels about me."

"You think he would do what he did for you if he didn't feel ya."

"Nah but you don't know Money. If he likes you as a friend then nobody can cross you and get away with it. So what he did for me today, he would do for you tomorrow if he considers you a friend."

"Well my advice to you is to show him you're the one and see how he reacts. But that means no more of these Ricky dudes. Remember this, a man may not say you're his but if you play the part sooner or later, he'll lay claim."

"Thank you, Uncle Sha."

"Don't sweat it. Now, let's go get something to eat."

CHAPTER 2

"So what's the deal, kid? You ain't said two words since we left."

"I know but shit about to get real sweet and serious and I needed a minute to grasp everything I was told."

"Well what's up with that work?"

"As of Friday, it's on and popping. We getting 50 kilos of that pure shit at 10 g's a brick."

"What! Are you kidding me?"

"Nah dawg. This shit is for real. He also said that his nephews would be coming here to handle any problems that we might need to be dealt with."

"You didn't tell him we don't need no help!"

"I did but after thinking about it, it might not be such a bad idea after all."

"How's that?"

"Think about it. We said we wouldn't fuck with niggas from around here because we know they can be grimy but now we can have three homeboys that ain't from here and we don't have to worry if we can trust them because if he trusts them then that makes them trustworthy."

"Yeah, you right but we still better keep an eye on them."

"Oh I wouldn't have it any other way."

When Friday came around T-Money and Strapp were sitting at T-Money's mom's house waiting on a phone call from Slim T.

"Terry, you and Tony want something to eat?"

"No thank you, mama. We just waiting on Slim T to call."

"Who?"

"Tiesa, mama."

"Oh. I told you about using all those street names all the time."

"I'm sorry mama."

"Well if y'all change your minds there's some hamburgers on the stove."

"Okay mama."

"Man, I don't know about you but I'm starving, Money."

"Grab something to eat. I don't feel like it."

"You alright, kid? I ain't never known you to turn down no food, especially from Mrs. Hampton, you know she be throwing down."

"Oh trust me; I'll punish something later on. I just want to get this business out the way first."

"I feel you kid but in the meantime I'm about to fuck a couple of these burgers up."

"Watch your mouth kid."

"Oh my bad dawg."

"Don't even sweat it."

It was about 7:30 that evening before they finally got the call. Ring, ring, ring.

"Damn baby girl, I thought y'all left the country."

"Stop playing silly and come on over."

"Alright, give us about ten minutes."

"Okay. I'll see you then."

"Alright, peace out."

"Was that him?"

"Yeah that was him. He said he'll be here in about ten minutes."

"Good. We finally get to meet Mr. T-Money."

"Why you say it like that?"

"Oh, it ain't nothing. It's just that Uncle Sha said he reminds him of himself when he was coming up. And you know if he said that then he must really like dude."

"Well I couldn't tell and he didn't say anything to me about T-Money."

"You of all people should know sometimes he'll say and sometimes you have to know."

Knock, knock, knock. "Come on in."

"What did I tell you about that come on in shit?"

"But Money, I knew it was you."

"I don't give a damn what you think you know you can never be too sure."

"My bad, Money."

"Don't even sweat it just don't let it happen no more."

"Okay. What's up, Strapp?"

"Ain't nothing. You know me just chillin' like a villain."

"I heard that."

"Well y'all come on and let me introduce y'all to the fam."

"T-Money, Strapp, these are my cousins Young World, Ratt and Wreckless." After everybody introduced Slim T excused herself so the boys could get down to business.

"So Money, what's good with ya?" Young World asked as he was rolling a blunt.

"Ready to get this paper and take this shit to a new level."

"Well in that case, Ratt show the man what he working with!"

"Here ya go playa; the purest shit this side of the border." When T-Money saw the flakes in the kilo he knew this was some grade A shit.

"Like what you see?" Wreckless asked.

"Hell yeah!"

"Good. Now let's discuss why we are here."

After talking for several hours, T-Money had a full grasp of everything. Young World, who was the youngest of the three, was who T-Money had decided he would take under his wing sort of like a little brother. And at 6 foot and 1 inch, tall dark complexion and a natural 180 pounds rip up with hair that went just below his shoulders, catching the ladies' eyes shouldn't be a problem. And while the appearance didn't show it T-Money could sense the killer that was within him. Now Ratt on the other hand was another case. You could tell at first glance that you were dealing with a maniac. He had the eyes of a killa and yet the persona of a pimp. Although he didn't look like a ladies man, Money was quite sure he had his way with the ladies. Last but not least was Wreckless, at about 6 feet 2 inches tall, he and Ratt stood about the same height. If one was listening and not looking you wouldn't know the difference. Even their weight was similar at around the 200 pound mark, but in areas where Ratt was not solid Wreckless was. While Ratt was a darker complexion, Wreckless was a few shades lighter. It was learned in the early conversation that both, Ratt and Wreckless, earned their names because of the damage they could cause. So in all what you had was a group of young killers with the attitude and personalities to match.

"Well boys, it's been real for the moment and we'll be in touch in a couple of days but right now we gonna try and make a few paper moves."

"Alright." Young World said. "But remember we just a phone call away."

"True dat." Then T-Money and Strapp left.

"What y'all think?"

"I like his style." Ratt said.

"Yeah, me too." Said Wreckless. "What about you World?"

"I think we met a real nigga about real business and we about to make some major paper."

"Well Slim T, looks like your boy is the real deal. What's up with y'all two anyway?"

"We been kind of just kicking it."

"If you know like I know you better try to be wifey."

"Why you say it like that, Wreckless? You know I already got cheese."

"It ain't the money even though that's never a bad option. It's just something about him that seems right."

"Well only time will tell, won't it?"

"Sure will."

"It sure will."

"Damn, Money, you the fucking man!" Strapp said after looking at 50 kilos for the first time in his life.

"Ain't no 'you' in we, homie."

"So that means we the men."

"Remember if I got you got and that's for life, homie. Now can you think of anybody trying to get their weight up?"

"You know ain't shit in the streets so we can get about 25 a brick with ease."

"Hell at this price we can lock the city down. And then the good thing is it's that grade A shit, no cut or nothing."

"Since it's like that I know just who to holla at." Said Strapp. "Let me see the phone."

"Nah remember no B.I. (business) over the cells, only at the pay phones. Remember we running shit so if somebody ain't on our time then fuck 'em!"

"Damn straight, playa! Well in that case pull this motherfucker over."

Ring, ring, ring. "Yeah what's up?"

"Let me holla at Pimping Slim."

"This is him."

"Hey man, it's Strapp."

"Oh, what's up with you, kid?"

"I'm straight but the question is are you straight?"

"Man, you know it's a motherfucking drought! Ain't nobody got shit. And the few people I do know they done stepped on that shit so much it won't even come back."

"Well guess what playa."

"What's happening?"

"I got some white girl that got that come-back and it's a money back on that pussy."

"Oh yeah."

"Damn straight."

"How much she want for that pussy?"

"For you, 25 a shot."

"Well then you need to come holla at your boy. I might just trick about 20 of them hoes."

"In that case give me about 15 minutes and I'll be there."

"Word. I'll be waiting."

"What's up, Strapp?"

"Oh man, we in business. I know this cat, we call Pimping Slim, moved down here from Jack Town (Jackson, Mississippi)."

"What he want?"

"Oh dude trying to buy 20 of them things."

"Well what did you tell him?"

"I told him 25 thousand a brick."

"When he want it?"

"I told him we would be there in 15 minutes."

"Okay we'll wait for about 30 minutes and then go."

"Why 30 minutes?"

"Because in the game on time could be the last time, but slow money is good money."

"That's why I'm glad you on my team because you always thinking."

"That's why we're a team because two heads is always better than one."

About 30 minutes later, T-Money and Strapp pulled up outside of Pimping Slim's house.

"Strapp, how long you been knowing this nigga?"

"About 3 years Money, why what's up?"

"Well I was going to let you handle this yourself but we talking about half a mill ticket and I know some niggas that would kill they mamas for that of cheese."

"Oh no doubt Homie."

"If he wants to deal it's both of us or nothing."

"And besides 4 guns are better than two."

Knock, knock, knock. "Sheena, get the door."

"Ok." When the door opened T-Money was in shock. Before him stood one of the prettiest women he had ever seen.

"What's up Strapp?"

"What's up Sheena?"

"This here is my man T-Money."

"Well hello there, Mr. Money. Please come in."

"Thank you."

"Who is it, Sheena?"

"You know who it is nigga." Strapp said as they bent the corner.

"What's good, kid?"

"Just chillin' trying to live. By the looks of this crib I'd say you're living pretty good."

"Who you got with you, kid?"

"This here is my cousin T-Money."

"Okay. What's up T-Money?"

"Ain't nothing, just chillin'."

"Well Strapp, let's get down to business. Right this way." When T-Money tried to follow another big dud about 6 feet 4 inches tall and about 260 pounds stood up and said, "Just him." Referring to Strapp.

"I'm sorry partner but I go where the goods go and that's non-negotiable." It was at this time that T-Money showed what lay behind his cool demeanor (a killer). With the next motion the big guy was looking down the barrel of T-Money's two Desert Eagles.

"Now Pimping Slim, is it? Unless you're ready to redecorate the interior with a dark shade of red I suggest you tell your fake ass bodyguard to sit the fuck down!"

"Big, just chill out, it's all good. You got to respect a man looking out for his people or his product." Money didn't say nothing because he knew Pimping Slim was trying to find out whose dope it was. Unknowing to all the men in the house, Sheena was watching from where she stood in the hallway. Seeing this stranger handle Big the way he did really turned her on, but what really had her pussy pulsating was the calm demeanor in which he did it. And it was at that time when Sheena decided she would have to sample this product!

"Now fellas, can we get back to business?"

"Oh trust me, Slim, it's always business and it's never personal."

Strapp gave Slim a kilo which he in return gave to Big. "You know what to do. Let me know what you got." Big went upstairs where his uncle was.

"Here Unc, see what we working with." Big's uncle broke a piece off and put it in his glass dick and began to suck. It wasn't five seconds before he started choking and coughing, nodding his head in approval.

"Man Big, this is that fire! Tell Slim this is the real deal. It has to be about 92 percent pure."

"Alright, I'll holla at you later."

"Well Big, what did Unc say?"

"He said this was the real deal about 92 percent pure."

"No shit!"

"That's what he says, well you know after 20 years of that shit he knows what he's talking about."

"Well fellas, looks like we got a deal and I hope we can continue to do business in the immediate future, like say tonight?"

"In that case I'll hit you up tonight and you can tell me what you want."

"Okay, well T-Money, it was nice meeting you and I apologize for your trouble."

"Oh no problem but if you want my advice you better get you some real killers on your team for security because he's not made for this! Trust me I can see it in his eyes and the next time I will kill him."

While leaving, T-Money noticed a note that was left on the windshield.

"What's that Money?"

"Oh just another back I need to dig out."

"Damn boy, you're like a magnet for pussy."

"Hey what can I say, pimping ain't easy but someone's got to do it. So why not me?" With that being said both of them laughed as they pulled off.

CHAPTER 3

Because T-Money and Strapp was known in the streets and the prices were low compared to what people were used to paying, the dope was selling like crazy. And with it being a drought it was extra sweet. In one month's time they had sold over 300 kilos. T-Money brought his mother a brand new house through his uncle. Since his uncle had a legit construction company it wouldn't look funny. Strapp also purchased his mother a house that was two houses down from T-Money's mother's house. This way when one of them checks on his mother, he could also check on the other. T-Money also purchased himself a condominium in the next town over (Gainesville, Fl.). The only difference was no one knew this but his mother and him. Even though Strapp is his best friend he knew in the game the right hand never lets the left hand know everything and that's just the way it is!

Ring, ring, ring. "What's up?"

"Hey Strapp, where you at?"

"I'm at mom's crib."

"Okay cool. I'm going to come by and get you so we can go handle that."

"Alright playa. Hit the horn when you get out front."

"Nah, just be waiting for me."

"Why you can't hit the horn?"

"It's not that I can't but it's disrespectful to your moms. And besides its 10:30 in the morning, you should be up anyway."

"Okay dad. I'll be waiting."

"Alright, peace out."

Early in the week T-Money had arranged the sale of four black on black H2 Hummers, one for each member of his crew. Not even Strapp knew where they were really going because he thought when T-Money went to pick up the boys that it had something to do with business and even though Uncle Sha was paying the boys for the work they were apart of T-Money's crew so he wanted to look for everyone. Besides that no one had a car but T-Money's 91 Box Chevy and Slim T's Acura Coupe. Now that business was doing good they could hang like real boys, not to mention that it was time to make a few booty calls since it's been all business. And you know what they say about all business and no pleasure.

"Shit man! I thought you said you would be here in a few minutes."

"I did but you know I'm never on time."

"Whatever, let's go do this because I got a little ass lined up for tonight."

"Uh oh, you getting your nuts out of pawn?"

"Ha, ha, ha, very funny motherfucker. I might not be no dicksman like you but trust me I'll dig a bitch back out quick."

"I heard that. I'm going to do me a little pussy popping myself tonight."

"It's about time nigga! I thought you had started fucking the money."

"Oh you got jokes, huh?" And with that the boys drove to Slim T's house.

"Hey Young World, you know where T-Money taking us this early in the morning?"

"First of all, hell nah, and second it's not early."

T-Money

"The hell if it ain't! You know I like to sleep until about 1 pm."

"Man Wreckless, stop crying about some sleep."

"It ain't that, I need some pussy! All we been doing is going back and forth with that dope. Now don't get me wrong the money Uncle Sha is paying us is the shit but we need to enjoy it too."

"Now that's what I'm talking about." Ratt said. "We need not you but we need some motherfucking pussy!"

"Well here goes T-Money and Strapp. Maybe they'll hook us up when we get back from wherever it is we're going."

"What's up, fellas? Y'all ready to roll?"

"Yeah, we ready Money but we need to ask you one question."

"Oh, what's that?"

"When we gonna get some pussy?"

"Oh you ain't said nothing Ratt. Just wait until we come back and I promise we will have all the pussy you guys can stand."

"Well in that case, let's roll out!" When the guys rolled out Slim T just looked out the window wondering when she would get T-Money all to herself. Yeah she knew he was making money but tonight she was determined to be in the right place at the right time.

"Damn Money, you got deals going on with somebody at the Hummer lot?"

"Yeah so I'm going to need all of y'all on this one."

"You think it might be some bullshit about to pop off?"

"Yeah so Strapp you and boys stay ready."

"Hell yeah!" Ratt said. "It's about time we got to put in some motherfucking work."

"You ain't never lied." Wreckless said. "Let's get this shit popping."

As the group of five headed towards the entrance a middle aged white salesman named Frank approached them. "Hello fellas, what can I do for you?"

"My name is T-Money. Is Mr. Nelson in?"

"Yes he is but can I be of some help?"

"Hell fuck nah!" Young World said. "Not unless your name is Mr. Nelson. And if it's not then you need to go get him and stop running your mouth."

"Okay sir. One moment please."

"Oh scary ass white man probably thinks we want to rob this place."

"Oh they don't think that. Trust me!"

"Hey there, Money. What's good with you?"

"Nothing too much, Mr. Nelson. Just here to do a little business."

"Well in that case come right this way." T-Money knew he was playing it close. He had four trigger happy gangsters with him and if anything goes wrong he could have a blood bath on his hands. So it was time to get it over with.

"Well here they go, Money. I hope you guys enjoy."

"What the fuck is he talking about?" Strapp said.

"Oh, he's just talking about these four Hummers I brought y'all."

"Man, get the fuck out of here!"

"Nah Ratt, I'm dead serious. As a matter of fact the keys are in them. I'll meet you guys back at Slim T's house in a couple hours."

"Hey, where you going to Money?"

"I'm going to knock the dust off my dick. It's been a while."

"Oh don't be fronting! You're about to knock the dust off your tongue too."

"Oh ain't no question about that but the head ain't never rusty so peace out."

When T-Money got back in his car he reached in the glove compartment and pulled out the note that was left on the car by the woman at Pimping Slim's house. Phone in hand he dialed the number on the note. "Hello."

"Um, yes. May I speak to Sheena?"

"This is She."

"Well, how are you doing this morning baby girl?"

"And just who is this I'm talking too?"

"Well, being that you left me the note I would assume that you would be expecting my call."

"Oh, okay. This is Mr. T-Money right?"

"The one and only."

"And to what do I owe this pleasant surprise?"

"It's been a while since I've had the companionship of a lady and I thought maybe you could help me get in touch with that side of me again."

"That's a good possibility."

"Well just tell me what I need to do to make this happen and it's as good as done."

"Oh, it's like that?"

"No doubt!"

"First of all, I am a lady so I'll tell you up front that I don't do hotels and secondly, are you yourself as a person going to be with my time?"

"Only time will tell. Now is that all?"

"Last but not least I'm tired of my situation so if you can put me in a different one then holla at me."

"I'll be there in ten minutes."

"And I'll be waiting."

"Alright. Peace out." Now having been a vet in the game, T-Money knew exactly what this meant. Sheena was tired of the dick she had and was looking for a new one, which pretty much confirmed that this was Big's woman. For one Pimping Slim had millions and with that kind of money it would take more than a good looking man that you saw and a poor sex life. Besides that, for her to pull a bold move like this, that means that she doesn't think much about the dude.

"I was starting to think you weren't coming."

"One thing you can always count on is my word. Regardless of what the odds are if I say I'm going to do something then you can expect it!"

It only took about 20 minutes to reach T-Money's crib once they were on the highway. He made it seem like he had a surprise for her but truth be told he didn't want her to know where he stayed at. Once they were there he led her in the house and said, "Okay you can take it off now!"

"Damn! You have one hell of a place here. Do you stay here all alone?"

"Yes, as a matter of fact I do but who knows you could change that."

"Oh really?"

"Trust me if I say it then it can be done. So tell me Sheena, who's situation was you in? Pimping Slim's or Big's?"

"Why do I get the feeling you already know the answer to that? But to answer your question: Big!"

"And just how did a lovely young lady like yourself make that mistake?"

"To tell you the truth I really don't know. I guess being young we all make some mistakes. I was only 15 when I met him and he made everything sound so perfect. But for three years it's been anything but perfect. But I'm not mad because I've seen and learned too much and I don't know if given the right situation I can be that ride or die bitch and the lady that any man would love to have."

"You know Sheena; I can go for that because I've never seen you out."

"And you won't because the streets offer nothing but heartache and heartbreak and I'm not looking for either."

"So why are you here?"

"Because I know you haven't found what you're looking for. Because if you had she'd be your priority and the streets would be a second option."

"Oh and you got it like that?"

"Hell yeah! I already know that. It's up to you to find out."

"You know what Sheena, I like your style and I have been digging you since you first answered that door. Ever since then I've been wanting you."

"Well, you're not by yourself! So what do you say we pick this conversation up later and satisfy our wants and needs."

"I couldn't have said it better myself."

"Well guys, all y'all have to do is sign right here and the trucks are yours."

"Damn!" said Wreckless. "These joints are phat as hell and they're fully loaded with 7 T.V.'s, 6 15 inch speakers, 24 inch spinners, DVD player and phones in each steering wheel."

"Damn Strapp, I knew T-Money was straight but he on some real mob type shit."

"Yeah Ratt, one thing he believes in and that's looking out for his people."

"I see. I see. What's doing it for me is that I know he knows we can buy our own shit."

"That's just the type of dude he is, Young World."

"And before y'all leave, y'all will need these." At that time Mr. Nelson gave each of them a brand new driver's license.

"How in the fuck did he get these with our pictures and all?"

"Not even I know that Wreckless. I'd sure hate to be on his bad side."

"Wouldn't we all?" Said Strapp. "Wouldn't we all?"

While the boys were driving down the road back to back they had some unwanted eyes watching them. "Hey Rob, look at them niggas stunting."

"Yeah it's all good now but trust me they got it coming. Them and that fuck ass hoe Slim T."

"That's what's up my nigga."

"Oh you'll be surprised what you can learn when you fucking them hoes right. So like I said they got it coming and it's just a matter of time. All we gotta do is keep watching them niggas."

CHAPTER 4

T-Money and Sheena was just getting in the mood for what both hoped would be a night to remember. "Damn baby, you look good in panties and bra!"

"Well why don't you come and see if I feel as good as I look." When T-Money was in front of Sheena she looked him right in the eyes and kissed him seductively while stroking his manhood.

"Damn baby, is all that for me?"

"Yeah! And that's just the beginning." While Sheena was kissing him, T-Money slid her panties off and started finger fucking her wet pussy. "Ooh yes daddy, right there, right there daddy."

"Oh you like that?"

"Oh yes, T-Money. Shit that feels good." Turned on by his foreplay, Sheena dropped down to her knees and began to suck his dick and although she couldn't put it all the way in she was driving T-Money crazy.

"Oh yeah, that's it baby, suck that dick. Yeah, just like that baby, just like that!" T-Money didn't want to but knew if he didn't stop her he would never make it inside of her. "Aw fuck baby, I can't take it. Come here to daddy." As Sheena laid down on her back, T-Money spread her legs wide and placed them on his shoulders and slid his enormous dick in. "Ooh yes daddy, get this pussy. Get this pussy, daddy." Sheena continued to let out moans of pleasure. As her toes were curling, T-Money took and started sucking her toes. "Aww yeah baby, fuck me, fuck me, Money!"

"Tell me whose pussy this is!"

"It's your pussy, Money. It's your pussy." T-Money pulled his dick out and flipped Sheena over and began kissing all over her ass. He then spread her ass cheeks open and started circling her asshole with his tongue. "Ooh shit, baby! That's it baby, eat that ass, baby. Eat it!" T-Money then began sucking her pussy. "Oh baby I can't take it. I'm cumming baby, I'm cumming." When Sheena's knees grew weak and buckled, T-Money held her by her waist and started fucking her again. Sheena bit her lip as her eyes rolled in her head as she had one orgasm after another. "Oh shit, I'm cumming Sheena. I'm cumming."

"Cum daddy, cum for me daddy!" It was at that time he lost all control and collapsed on top of her.

All the fellas were at Slim T's house except T-Money. "Damn Strapp, ya boy must be really backed up!"

"Oh no doubt, the only thing he been doing is getting this money."

"Shit Ratt, you act like we don't need to get our nuts out of pawn. I'm horny as a motherfucker."

"Nah, I ain't tripping because Slim T said she was going to hook us up later on tonight."

"Oh, okay then! That's what I'm talking about."

"So all we got to do is chill and wait on T-Money. The rest is history."

"Hey Rob."

"What's up my man?"

"That bitch got things set up for tonight don't she?"

"Yeah as far as I know everything is going to go down about 9:00 tonight. All you got to do is make sure your cousins are ready."

"Oh trust me; them niggas is about handling their B.I."

"Well then at about 10:30 we should be counting money and breaking down bricks."

"How is she going to get them niggas to have all that money and dope on them?"

"Man I told you hoes can be the most slimiest bitches on the planet when they want to. So I don't know but I'm willing to bet that they will have it. And then when we get it we'll kill her ass too."

"Oh no doubt. I'll never let a bitch do me like she going to do these niggas."

While Slim T was driving home she had plenty of time to think about her upcoming actions. "I know after this T-Money better get his act together unless the same thing will happen to him that's about to happen to these wanna be gangsters and my Uncle Sha. After he raped me when I was 10, did he actually think it was going to be all gravy! But because of his guilt, he's allowed himself to get caught up in the most feared rule of the game: BETRAYAL. And I know Rob and Ski think I'm sprung but what better way to kill a nigga than with the element of surprise and as long as they think I don't know they want to kill me too, the better advantage I have."

After handling his business in bed, T-Money knew that sleep would come natural to Sheena. True, it had been a while but bedroom rules stay the same. First, always handle your business. Second, make a bitch bust more orgasms than you and last but not least, always let a bitch fall asleep first! But the game wasn't finished yet as T-Money was putting the icing on the cake.

"Good evening, Sleepyhead."

"Oh my God, what time it is Money?"

"It's about 5:30."

"In the morning?"

"No baby girl, in the p.m. I was going to wake you up earlier but you was sleeping too good."

"My bad, I hope I didn't disappoint you."

"Oh never that baby girl, it's just that so many dudes get caught up in the power of pussy that they forget about the power of the dick!"

"Ha, ha, ha, very funny Money."

"Nah but for real baby girl, I enjoyed myself. But listen; was you serious about a new situation?"

"As a heart attack."

"Okay, here's what you do. Go out to Marion Oaks today on 103rd Pine Hill Manor. When you get there a lady named Margie will meet you there with the keys."

"Is this another one of your homes?"

"Nah baby girl, just do like I told you and remember about that ride or die bitch you told me about Ms. Lewis."

"How…"

"What? How do I know your last name? Let's just say if it's in Ocala then I know about it. Now freshen up, get dressed and put that blind fold back on and let's roll."

Ring, ring, ring, ring. "What's up?"

"Goddamn Money, I know you needed to get your nuts out of pawn but shit!"

"Just chill Strapp, I'm on the way right now."

"Alright peace out."

"Hey Strapp, wait until I tell you about this shit."

"Oh Lord, not another freak fest."

"Yeah that too but that's just the beginning."

"Okay then, we all waiting for you."

"Is Slim T there too?"

"Yeah but she just got here about an hour ago. Besides I need to holla at you about something anyway."

"Alright I'll holla."

"Peace out."

After T-Money dropped Sheena off, she was all smiles. They had pulled up in a parking lot of the McDonalds beside a brand new 2005 Ford Mustang, black on black with jet black tints. Inside was a title with her name on it, Sheena Lewis, and it had a custom installed navigation system complete with MP3 player and four 10 inch speakers. When she pulled up to Pine Hill manor she was greeted by a tall white woman.

"Hi, my name is Margie and you must be Sheena."

"Yes ma'am."

"Well come on, let me give you the tour. This is a 4 bedroom house with 2 ½ bathrooms. The whole house has been designed with the top of the line equipment. There is a big screen in each of the rooms. Each bedroom has a Queen sized bed except the Master bedroom, where there is a King size bed. On the back patio there is a screened inn pool complete with a hot tub. There's a lake in the back which goes down ten miles just passed the Interstate on Highway 75 North."

"I don't think I need to know that much."

"Listen, Ms. Lewis, when it comes to Mr. Money, everything I tell you is important. Are we clear?"

"My bad."

"Don't mention it. Now downstairs is a game room and workout station but behind this game is a secret passage. Do you know how to ride a jet ski?"

"Yes. Why?"

"Well down the passage there are two jet skis just in case of an emergency. In the master bedroom there is a safe behind the picture on the wall with one hundred and fifty thousand dollars in it. Also in case of an emergency on the kitchen table you will find a Visa card with a thirty thousand dollar credit and ten thousand for you to get new clothes and whatever. As for your old situation, it's best to forget everything about him and realize the situation you're in now. Now all you have to do is sign here and forget I even exist. Oh and nobody is to know where you stay! If you need contact with your family or friends give them your cell phone number only."

"But I don't have a cell phone."

"It too is on the kitchen table. Oh and one last thing. When I leave call the number on the table and let it ring one time and then hang up and call back. Well Ms. Lewis, it was nice meeting you and hopefully you'll never see me again."

"Damn that bitch was nice nasty! And she had that same look in her eyes as T-Money when she made that last comment. But she better not get it twisted! I was born for this shit. I just needed the right nigga by my side. Trust me! Before long he'll know, I'm that bitch!"

CHAPTER 5

It was 6:30 p.m. when T-Money pulled up in front of Slim T's house. "Hey, what's up fellas?"

"Man, shit! You tell us, you the one been dusting off your nuts." Young World said.

"Feels like I just got out of prison if you know what I mean."

"Hell yeah! Ain't nothing like releasing a little pressure."

"All that's good Money." Ratt said. "But let me just say that was some real shit buying us them Hummers."

"Damn straight." Wreckless said. "But the real shit is how did you get the driver's licenses?"

"Let's just say to have money is an amazing thing but to be well connected is priceless."

"So what's up with that shipment?"

"Oh Slim T is supposed to have picked it up already but she ain't said shit since she's been back."

"Yeah." Young World said. "I don't know why Uncle Sha didn't just let us pick it up like always."

"Yeah, what's up with that?" Strapp asked.

"To tell you the truth Strapp, I really don't know but let me holla at you."

"Now what did you want to holla at me about?"

"I know you and Slim T alright but something's funny with that bitch!"

"Why do you say that?"

"I can't really put my finger on it but I don't trust her."

"I feel you because I don't trust her neither so we got to watch for the B.S."

"What's up Money?"

"Not too much baby girl. What's up with the shipment?"

"Oh it's all good. When I take the fellas to do their thing with the girls we'll pick it up."

"But why didn't you just let them pick it up in the first place? Isn't that part of the reason your uncle sent them!"

"Yeah but since you was out buying Hummers and shit, I just thought I would handle it and besides my uncle trusts me anyway."

"This is not about trust! This is business."

"Well, I'm not going to argue with you because I picked it up and what's done is done."

"You're right, my bad. Well, what do you have on the agenda for tonight?"

"I was hoping me and you could spend a little time together."

"Sounds like a plan to me."

"Well okay, you go in the house and get comfortable and I'll take the boys to meet the girls."

"What girls are you hooking them up with?"

"Tracie, Mary and two of their cousins."

"You ain't hooked us up with no rug rats, have you cuz?"

"Now Ratt, you know I don't even get down like that."

"In that case, let's be out."

"Okay Money, I'll see you when I get back."

"Alright."

"Strapp, hit me up when y'all headed back this way with the bricks."

"That's a bet Money."

"I'll holla."

When T-Money was in the house something kept nagging at him but he couldn't put his finger on it so he called Strapp. Ring, ring, ring. "Yeah, who is it?"

"It's me, Strapp."

"What's up, Money?"

"I got a bad feeling but I can't put my finger on it so watch yourself, dawg."

"No doubt, Money! I'm already on it."

"Okay then, I'll holla."

"Peace out."

The first stop Slim T made was to pick up the dope. "Okay Strapp, y'all hurry up and load that shit up so we can bounce."

"Just take it easy Slim T, pussy can wait. This shit here is business! Anyway how many is this?"

"It's 200 kilos just like it's supposed to be."

"Damn Strapp, you need to slow your roll talking to my motherfucking cousin like that." Wreckless said. "Who you think you is? T-Money?"

"Oh, it's like that?"

"Hell yeah when it comes to our blood." Ratt said.

"Man, y'all need to chill the fuck out." Young World said. "Strapp is right. This is business! We been waiting on pussy all this time a few more minutes won't hurt to make sure everything is good."

"So what you saying, Young World? You think Uncle Sha shorted the package?"

"I ain't saying shit! All I know is if you pay for something you want to make sure it's what you paid for. Oh and just in case you forgot, Slim T, don't forget my dawg paid for one hundred of them thangs up front."

"And that hundred goes with me." Strapp said.

When Slim T saw the tension that was building up, she knew she had to calm it down. If not she knew for a fact that Strapp would kill or die for T-Money. But the funny thing was that Young World seemed to side with Strapp but none of it mattered because they were all going to die tonight. Then it would be just her and T-Money or just her and the dope. Either way, she would win.

"Okay fellas, let's just calm down. We all on the same team so let's just get finished."

When they were finished loading up the dope they went straight to Tracie's house.

"Okay fellas, the girls are waiting."

"They already know what's going down so when y'all get finish y'all can meet us back at my house, alright?"

"Hey Slim T, are these the boys?"

"Yeah this is the crew."

"Well boys let's get this party started."

"Alright fellas, I'm out."

"Alright Ski, tell your cousins to wait until the hoes get finished doing their thang and then when the girls come out that's when we go in."

"One nigga to every room so make sure they handle their B.I."

"Well boys, these are the girls. This is Mary. This is Tasha. And this is Shelly. All y'all have to do is choose which one you want and have a good time." Wreckless was the first to get up.

"I'll take this one right here." As Tasha stood up she was more than an eye full. She was built like Serena Williams, only better looking. Ratt was next as he choose Shelly. Shelly was the model type, tall, pretty and full of curves. Last but not least was Mary. Now Mary was very attractive. She was about 5 feet 8 inches tall with measurements of 24-36-24.

"Well, I guess I'm all yours."

"Let's do this." Young World said.

"Tracie, where is the one for you?"

"Oh he's coming. He had to make a call."

"Don't worry about me, Mary. You better try to focus on that fine motherfucking young buck ready to go deep in you."

"I know girl, ain't he fine?"

"Well, I'll see you later Tracie."

"Okay, handle your business."

"Ooh yeah, Shelly, suck that dick. That's right, deep throat that dick, bitch!"

"Ooh baby, I want you to put that big dick in this wet pussy. Please, please, fuck me baby."

Ratt laid Shelly down on the bed and gave her a little surprise first. "Oh, don't stop! Don't stop, baby! Suck that pussy good. Ooh Ratt, you gonna make me cum."

When Ratt heard that he stopped sucking her pussy. He then turned her on her stomach and began fucking her slowly.

In the other room, Wreckless was putting in work! "Ooh big boy, talk dirty to me while you're in this hot pussy."

"Tell Daddy whose pussy this is."

"Ooh big daddy, this is your pussy."

"Whose?"

"Your pussy."

"Tell me what you want!"

"Awww, ooh, aww, ooh fuck this pussy, daddy! Fuck this pussy."

"Oh shit girl, I'm gonna cum."

"No daddy, don't cum, don't cum."

"Oh shit, I'm exploding. Ah yeah, ooh that felt so good."

"Ooh yes! Lick that pussy, you young stud. Ooh fuck, that feels good. Ooh yeah, spit in that pussy baby, oh fuck I'm cumming! I'm cumming, boo!"

Young World kept sucking that pussy while Mary came in his mouth driving her out of her mind. He then spread her legs apart and slid his dick in her drenched pussy.

"Ooh yeah, fuck me baby! Fuck me with that young hard dick." While Mary was moaning, Young World put her big toe in his mouth and began sucking it.

"Oh fuck, baby! What are you doing to me?" I'm cumming, I'm cumming baby!"

"Tell me the world is mine!"

Strapped

"The world is yours babbbby. The world is yours. Ooh baby, I'm cumming again, daddy. I'm cumming again."

"Hey Rob, y'all ready?"
"Hell nah, Ski. We got to wait until them hoes come out."
"For what? Let's kill them bitches too."
"Hell nah, dumb ass nigga! Slim T said if we kill the girls we don't get shit."
"Yeah but ain't we gonna kill her ass, too?"
"Yeah, but we got to get the dope first."
"Okay, I feel you."
"So let's wait about 15 more minutes and then it's on!"

Ring, ring, ring. "Hello!"
"Money, what's up?"
"Who is this?"
"This is Strapp dawg."
"Damn dawg, the pussy was that good you couldn't wait until you got here."
"Hell no, dawg! Now listen to me. I think the bitch Slim T is trying to set us up."
"Why you think that?"
"For one the bitch was tripping about the bricks. She didn't want me to count them or nothing."
"Oh yeah."
"Hell yeah. Why the fuck you sounding all calm and shit?"
"Think about it!"
"Oh okay, she right there with you."
"Now you got it. But hey, check this, I'm gonna hit you back in about two minutes."
"Alright Money."

T-Money had put the sex down on Slim T and the bitch was asleep with her arm across him so he slid out the bed and went into the bathroom.

Ring, ring, ring. "Yeah, what's up?"
"Did you tell the guys?"
"Nah!"
"Why not?"
"For one, I never went in the house and for two; Ratt and Wreckless kind of tried me about checking Slim T about the B.I."
"You say them two, well what about Young World?"
"The kid had my back! That's why it didn't get ugly because you know I get down for mines."
"Well look, call him and tell him to get out the house."
"What about the other two?"
"If he can warn them, fine. If not then too fucking bad."
"What you gonna do with the bitch?"
"Oh don't worry. I'm gonna tie her ass up until we find out what's happening alright."
"Alright, I'll holla back."

Meanwhile Young World wasn't ready for the shit he was about to hear. But in the game they say expect the unexpected. "Hey, what's your name?"

"Just call me Young World."

"Well I need you to listen to me and pay close attention because a lot depends on it."

"Okay I'm listening."

"Well first of all I'm glad you chose me because I been digging you since I first seen you. But anyway, Slim T is setting y'all up to get killed."

"What!"

"Please keep it down and listen. When we come out the rooms some guys are supposed to come in and kill y'all and take the dope y'all just picked up."

"Who are the guys?"

"Some guys named Rob and Ski."

"And they got two more guys with them."

Ring, ring, ring. "Yeah, what's up?"

"Hey World, I need you to get out of that house right now!"

"Yeah I know."

"What do you mean?"

"I'll tell you later. What part of the house are you in?"

I never came in. Well look its some guys in the house waiting on the girls too come out and then kill us."

"What the fuck!"

"I don't know where Ratt and Wreckless are at."

"Well don't leave the room. I'm coming in to get you."

"Do you know it's four of them?"

"Well you got your heat on you right?"

"Oh no doubt!"

"Well all we can do I hope they got theirs because I'm coming to get you!"

"Hey wake up, bitch!"

"What, what's wrong with you? And why you got me tied up?"

"Well first of all why don't you start by telling me what you got going on?"

"What are you talking about?"

"Oh you don't know!"

"Hell no, nigga! Now take this motherfucking rope off of me!"

"Well that's not going to happen right now."

"Why?"

"Because I'm waiting on a few calls to decide your fate."

"Ooh wait until I tell my uncle."

"No need, I already did that and he wants me to call him back when I find out what's the deal. So if you got any favors with God you better call them in."

CHAPTER 6

Ring, ring, ring. "Yeah, what's up?"

"Hey man, this is Strapp. You ain't gonna believe this shit that just went down."

"What in the hell happened, Strapp?"

"The bitch Slim T tried to have us killed!"

"What!"

"Yeah but you need to get to the hospital."

"Why, what happened?"

"Wreckless got shot."

"Alright Strapp, I'll meet you there."

"Alright. But hey, Money."

"Yeah, what's up?"

"Keep that bitch alive because I need to see her." T-Money could tell by the sound of Strapp's voice that whoever crossed his path now would have a better chance with HIV!

"Damn, this shit is fucked up, Strapp!"

"Oh trust me, Young World, before this is over somebody else will be fucked up too."

"Yeah, but why the hell would Slim T go out like that? She had to know that betrayal to Uncle Sha is death."

"Man, your Uncle Sha is the last person she has to worry about right now."

"Why you say that?"

"Because in the situation she's in right now death is already on her mind."

"Oh, y'all already knew what was going on?"

"Not really. The reason I didn't come in the house was because I've never trusted Slim T."

"Why is that?"

"Remember how she was tripping earlier about me taking half the dope?"

"Yeah, well we got to the girls' house she didn't say anything else about the dope. Now don't forget we in a wide open house with no fence or security so if you was tripping before you should definitely be tripping about that!"

"I never even looked at it like that."

"And then why would she want us to pick up the dope while we going to trick some hoes? Why not just wait until we get finish to pick it up on the way back home? So I called T-Money and told him and he tied her ass up while she was sleeping. Now all we got to do is question her ass when we get there."

"I can't wait!"

"Excuse me, sir."

"Who the fuck you talking too?"

"Just calm down we just to ask you a few questions."

"Man, who the fuck are y'all?"

"My name is Agent Harris and this is my partner Agent Smith. We're with the F.B.I."

"What the fuck y'all want to ask me about?"

"Ain't you the one who brought the gunshot victim in?"

"And what if I did?" Ratt asked. "Is it against the law to do that?"

"No, but with the severity of the wound we need to ask you a few questions."

"Well, ask them so y'all can get the fuck out my face!"

"Hey Young World, you think you gonna be alright?"

"Yeah, I'm fine but I ain't going in with you."

"That's a good idea because you know somebody called the police."

"I know. But you go ahead and check out Wreckless and I'll see you when you come out."

"Alright, be easy."

"Hey Strapp, hold on."

"Damn Money, you got here fast."

"Yeah, I just left that bitch tied up until we leave from up here. So what the hell happened?"

"When we got to the hoes' house, she wasn't tripping no more about the dope. And the more I thought about it things just didn't make sense. Like why would we pick up a package while we going tricking? It would make more sense to pick it up on the way back. But I didn't know the bitch was this slimy! Why the fuck would she do that anyway, Money?"

"I don't know because the bitch got money! And on top of that it's her uncle's shit. But I don't think it's about the dope. Whatever it is she'll tell it when we get back, trust me!"

After asking Ratt one hundred questions, Agents Harris and Smith weren't any closer from the time they began. "So, that's all you can tell us?"

"No that's all he's gonna tell us." Agent Smith said.

"Man, fuck y'all crackers. I ain't got nothing else to say to y'all."

"Oh, we'll see you again."

"Not if I can help it."

As Ratt was still fussing with the FBI, T-Money and Strapp walked up.

"What's the deal homie?"

"These pussy ass crackers asking me all these questions instead of trying to find out who shot my nigga!"

"And who are you?"

"Nah the question is do you like your job? Because if not I'm sure my lawyer can file a couple harassment suits that if you don't lose your job then you'll be directing traffic for a long time."

"Well Mr., I didn't catch your name."

"That's because I didn't give it to ya."

"Well anyway, I'm Agent Harris and this is Agent Smith and we're trying to gather any information that would be helpful in this shooting."

"First of all, I'm quite sure the gentleman has told you all he knows and second nobody here is a snitch so my suggestion to you is to beat your feet."

"Excuse me!"

"In other words step the fuck off!"

"You know we could have you arrested for disorderly conduct?"

"What's that a $50.00 bond, go ahead, make my fucking day."

When they saw T-Money was worse than Ratt they decided to call it quits and wait for something to break.

"Goddamn hood rats always want to be tough." Agent Smith said.

"Don't worry about it, partner, they'll mess up and when they do we'll be there."

"Yeah because they know more than what they're saying. Especially that first guy."

"You're right but it's the second guy that I worry about."

"Why is that?"

"Because when he came the first guy didn't say another word and that bothers me."

"Man, what the fuck are the feds doing here?" Strapp asked.

"Well anytime it's a shooting the hospital has to call the po-po."

"Yeah, the police I understand, but the Feds?"

"It is kind of funny but they don't have shit so fuck 'em."

"How can you be so sure?" Ratt asked.

"I can't right now but I will trust me. In the meantime, let's go check on Wreckless and then go find out what's up with this bitch and why she tried to have us killed."

"Are you going to call Uncle Sha?"

"Yeah as soon as we leave up out of here."

"Excuse me; are y'all the family of the patient just brought in?"

"Is he okay?" T-Money asked.

"I'm sorry but he didn't make it."

"No, no, no, no, no. He can't be dead." At that time, Ratt just fell down and started crying.

"Come on homie, he's gone to a better place."

"Fuck man! Wreckless was like my brother man."

"I know dawg, but as long as I'm living you always got family and that's my word and I don't break that for no one!"

Back at Slim T's house, she was trying to get loose but T-Money had tied her up good. "Damn, I can't get these ropes off! I wonder what could have went wrong. It won't matter if they find out I was behind all of this. All I can do is pray they don't find out."

While leaving the hospital, it was a lot of tension in the air. They had stopped and picked up Mary from where they dropped her off at and were now headed back to Slim T's house.

"Man, whoever is behind all of this is one dead ass!" Ratt said.

"Oh don't worry, we about to find out some answers in a few minutes. Oh we know who did this. Yeah thanks to Mary right there and Strapp we know."

"Well, who the fuck is it?"

"Slim T."

"What!"

"Yeah Slim T tried to have y'all killed."

"How the hell you figure that?"

"After y'all had sex with the girls, they were supposed to leave out the rooms and let the dudes come in."

"Well what happened?"

"For one thing, Strapp didn't trust her so he never came in."

"Well that ain't saying much."

"I'm gonna tell you something, Ratt. When you know somebody like I know Strapp you get a feel for them and their strong points. And his intuition is as good as it comes. Then secondly, Mary told Young World what was going down when they were in the room."

"Oh, so y'all gonna take the word of some trick ass bitch over my cousin's?"

"Well, we are about to ask Slim T ourselves and then you can see for yourself."

CHAPTER 7

T-Money could see this wasn't going to go well with Ratt so he knew he would have to do this the hard way. So he pulled over at the gas station. "Hey Strapp, go pay for the gas?"

"How much?"

"Fill it up."

"Y'all want something out of here, Young World?"

"Nah, I'm good."

"Okay, I'll be right back." When Strapp went in the store he just sat down at one of the tables.

"What's the deal, Money?"

"How did you know I wanted to holla at you?"

"First of all, like you told Ratt, I been knowing you for years. Secondly, the tank is already on full."

"Boy, you're good but check this. When we get out the truck I want you to knock Ratt out. That way we can tie him up too and then call Uncle Sha."

"You ain't said nothing because I been wanting to do that anyway."

They were so busy thinking about the ongoing events that they didn't even notice they were being followed.

"All we got to do Agent Smith is keep following them and sooner or later, they'll mess up. And when they do we'll be right there to have the last laugh."

"It's about time we got here." Ratt said. "Now we can find out the truth." Whop, whop.

"What the fuck are you doing, Strapp?"

"I told him to do it, Young World. I'm quite sure you can see that he wasn't cooperating. And if he couldn't stand us suspecting Slim T with cold hard evidence, he sure wasn't going to like seeing her tied up."

"Tied up!"

"Yeah just until we find out what Uncle Sha wants to do."

When they entered the house, Slim T was still struggling trying to get loose. "It's about time you brought your ass back Money. Now untie me."

"First Young World has a few questions for you."

"Young World!"

"Yeah or did you think he'd be dead by now. Oh and guess who else is here?"

"What the fuck are you talking about?"

"We brought Mary by to holla at you, too."

"Slim T, come on cuz, tell me this isn't true. Tell me it's been a mistake."

"Young World, I don't know what they're talking about."

"Stop lying Slim T! Just tell them the truth and maybe they'll let you go."

"Bitch! Who the fuck you think you talking to? You got some good dick and now you're Ms. Righteous!"

"No! But I ain't never tried to kill nobody."

"And me neither, bitch!"

"Okay, then how do I know about the 200 kilos? And how your Uncle Sha would trust you to pick it up because you had something on him. And don't forget while you talking about me sweating a good dick, T-Money's shit must be made of diamond because you said you was doing this so you and him could be together!"

"Hold the fuck up! You mean you tried to have us killed because Money was blowing your back out and he didn't want you. I should kill you my motherfucking self!"

"Fuck you, Young World! You don't know shit."

"I know my blood just tried to have me killed over a nigga's dick and that's fucked up!"

"What's fucked up is that when Uncle Sha was raping me there wasn't anybody there to help me."

"What!"

"Yeah, that's right; the uncle y'all look up to so much is a goddamn rapist."

"Well why didn't you say something?"

"Because I was scared."

"Oh you was scared to tell somebody about Uncle Sha but you wasn't scared to try and kill us!"

"Well apparently, it didn't work because you're still living."

"See, that's the fucked up part!"

"Why is that messed up?"

"Because Wreckless didn't make it. T-Money, what do you think we should do?"

"Well, first of all we need to call Uncle Sha."

"For what? I don't even want to see him."

"But listen Young World, Slim T has lied about so much why couldn't she by lying now?"

"You're right. Maybe we should just wait until we hear what he has to say."

"Now you're thinking because there's always two sides to every story. So, let's just wait it out."

The whole time this was going on in the house, Agent Smith and Harris was watching from outside. They had seen the big light skinned guy knock out the one who they were questioning and put him in the truck.

"Man, did you see that?"

"Yeah, you might want to see if this guy was a boxer or something to that effect."

"Well, what do you want to do Agent Smith?"

"It looks like they guy could be in some serious trouble if we don't help."

"Well, I guess we better go help then."

Ring, ring, ring. "Hello."

"Yeah, have you heard anything yet?"

"Yes we have but I can't address it over the phone."

"I kind of figured that so I'll be there in about 15 minutes."

"Well okay, but don't take too long because this thing gets real deep."

"Check and see if the door is open."

"Yeah, it's open."

"Okay, then let's take him out and put him in the back seat until he comes through."

"You think we should leave him tied up?"

"Yeah, that's probably a good idea. Hey, hurry up, I see some headlights coming."

As Agent Smith and Harris placed Ratt in the backseat, an all-black sedan pulled up and the driver got out and opened the door for another man in which they could not make out.

Knock, knock, knock. "Who is it?"

"It's Uncle Sha."

"The door's open. Come on in."

"Why would you just tell somebody to come in and not let them in?"

"Because if anybody can get through all this heat then he deserves to kill us." Strapp said.

"And what if it's the police?"

"Then we have a problem."

"My point exactly! So T-Money what have you found out?"

"The first thing is that your niece said you raped her when she was 9 or 10."

"What!"

"The next thing is that she tried to have them killed."

"Them who?"

"Strapp, Ratt, Young World and she succeeded with Wreckless."

"Wreckless is dead!"

"Yep."

"Slim T, what the fuck is wrong with you?"

"Don't try to act like you care about my well-being now. You didn't care when you was sticking your dick in my little young pussy!" Slap. Slap.

"How dare you disrespect me! I raised you. I made you and you wouldn't be shit if it wasn't for me!"

"But did that give you the right to rape her?"

"Don't tell me you believe this shit, Young World?"

"Well give me a reason why I shouldn't."

"Because I could have anything I want at any time."

"You have a point but why would she lie? She has to know that there's no way we could let her live after what she tried."

"I can't answer that because I'm just as shocked as you. But like you said she must be dealt with."

"Where's Ratt?"

"He's tied up in the truck."

"For what?"

"Because he didn't want to believe that Slim T was behind all of this."

"Well bring him in here so I can straighten him out."

"Oh, like you straightened me out, Uncle Sha?"

"I'm not going to entertain your foolishness anymore. T-Money bring Ratt in here."

"Strapp, go get him."

"Alright."

When Strapp got out to the truck he noticed that Ratt was not in the truck. He looked around for a minute not seeing anything he was headed back in the house. As he was headed back in the house he got a bad feeling and he turned around to look again.

"Hey Strapp, what's taking so long?" T-Money asked.

"That nigga ain't in the truck."

"What! Then where is he?"

"I don't know but hold on one second."

"Yeah, what's up, Strapp?"

"Take a look around for a minute and tell me what's wrong?" T-Money scanned the area with his eye and then he seen it.

"You see what I see Money?"

"No doubt. So let's just go back in the house and figure this shit out."

"Do you think they made us, Agent Smith?"

"It's hard to say. If they don't come out in about ten minutes then my guess is they're on to us."

"Man, what the hell is going on?"

"Agent Harris, look who just woke up?"

"Man, what the fuck y'all doing?"

"You should be glad to see us seeing as to how they had you tied up."

"They who?"

"The guys you rolled up with."

"Them motherfuckers!"

"Yeah and it was the big guy that was seated behind you that knocked you out."

"So, how did I end up with y'all?"

"Well, it didn't look so good for you so when they put you in the truck we took you out and put you in the car. Yeah you can go free anytime you want to but their intentions for you don't look good. But if you help us out then we might can help you."

"Hey y'all, we have a little problem."

"And what's that?" Uncle Sha asked.

"When Strapp went to get Ratt out the truck he wasn't there."

"Then where is he?"

"That we don't know but what Strapp and I saw was the same car that the agents from the hospital were in."

"You mean the Feds came to the hospital!"

"Yeah, they were trying to figure out what happened to Wreckless."

"This ain't good. We need to take care of this situation and chill out for a while."

"What we gonna do about Slim T?"

"We have to kill her." Young World said. "There's no way she can live because she knows too much and after a stunt like this that kills one of her cousins and tries to kill the other three, she can't be trusted."

"They know. I saw one of them look out the window."

"So what you want to do?"

"Y'all can just drop me off down the street."

"Are you sure?"

"Yeah, it's cool. I know what I got to do."

"Don't get yourself in anymore trouble."

"If y'all see me again it will be one of two ways. Either I'll be on lockdown for a long time or I'll be in a body bag!"

After seeing the agents pull off everybody knew it was business that needed to be handled. "Okay." T-Money said. "How are we going to handle this?"

"First, we need to kill Slim T!"

"And who's going to do that?"

"Not me." Young World said. "I know she pulled some low shit but I can't do it."

"Let me do it." Strapp said.

"Nah, I think I'll handle it!" T-Money looked Slim T in the eyes and the last words she heard were it's never personal, always business!

"What's next?" Young World asked.

"Well, we need to handle one more thing first."

"What's that?" Strapp asked. At that point everybody's eyes landed on Mary.

"No, no." Pop, pop, pop.

"Damn, why did we have to do that?" Young World asked.

"First of all," Uncle Sha said, "she is a key witness to all these murders. Second, anybody who will flip the game over a piece of dick ain't and can't be trusted!"

"What about Ratt?"

"From this point on, he is considered the enemy and should be handled as such. Trust me if he gets the chance he will do the same thing! Now let's clean this mess up and take care of these bodies."

"T-Money, you want me and World to bury them?"

"Nah, we don't want to take any chances of somebody finding them so we take them down to Alligator Alley and dump them out there."

When everything was taken care of Uncle Sha figured it would be best if everybody just chilled out for a while with the Feds trying to find out something. "Well, you guys just go on with your everyday life. If you haven't done nothing there's no reason to hide, so live."

After conversing for a while longer, Uncle Sha left. T-Money, Strapp and Young World talked a while longer. "I don't know about y'all," T-Money said "but I believe Slim T about Uncle Sha raping her."

"Me too." Young World said.

"What's up, Strapp?"

"First, I want y'all to be careful of that nigga, Ratt! He will be heated behind all of this and revenge will be his first agenda. Second, feed that nigga who just left here with a long handle spoon."

"Well, I'm leaving the country for a while." Young World said. "And I'll stay in touch."

"Listen, when you get where you're going, get a burn out phone. Just to be on the safe side. And what's up with you, Strapp?"

"Man, you know I'm a hood nigga. So I'm staying in the hood."

"Well, me, I'm going to chill for a while but y'all keep in touch."

After everybody said their peace they all went their separate way. T-Money hadn't kicked it with Sheena since he set her up in the house. For all he knew, she could be long gone with the money and all. If she was, it was her lost and not his. He had to admit that after that night with her he was feeling Sheena. She didn't know it and as a rule of the game he wouldn't expose his hand. And besides he had to make sure she was real with hers and down for his.

Reckless

CHAPTER 8

Ring, ring, ring. Knowing it could only be one person, she answered on key. "Hello Stranger, long time no see."

"Yeah, it's been kind of hectic out here so I've been handling mine."

"All that's good but can I have a little of your time?"

"As a matter of fact you can! How about for the next few days or months or years or whatever we just get to know each other."

"That sounds good but when do we start?"

"I'll be to the house in about 40 minutes. How's that?"

"That gives me just enough time to get ready for you and see if we can't make this house a home."

On the ride home, T-Money closed his eyes for a few minutes just to take everything in that had took place. After thinking for a while he knew that a vacation was just what he needed.

Young World was also in deep thought. After today's events he knew sometime in the future there would be no problems. He had called a friend named Sheila, who he had met on a cruise ship to the Bahamas and she was more than ready for his company. So he told her he'd be there late tonight and looked forward to his getaway.

Strapp was what most people considered a creature of habit. He never really did too much different because besides T-Money and now Young World, he was a loner. Yeah he had money but to the human eye you couldn't tell. He did this to blend in with his environment. He was very street smart and that in itself told him that after today there would be a price to pay. And when you look through the eyes of a killer often you find death around the corner!!

Ratt was truly heated. He knew in his heart that Slim T was dead. And if not for those agents he might have been dead. He would never believe Slim T set them up. But now he would never know. But he promised himself revenge! Young World, Strapp and T-Money himself would all die or he would die trying to kill them.

"Well Agent Smith, what do you think will happen now?"

"I can tell you a few things. One, betrayal is a deadly game within itself. Whoever betrayed the one they call Ratt, he will seek revenge. But because he doesn't know who betrayed him they're all his enemies. So there will be bloodshed and it's just a matter of time. But something went down in that house tonight, I'm sure. So tomorrow find out who lives there and let's pay them a visit."

"Baby girl, I'm home." T-money opened the door only to be met with the sweet sound of Alicia Keys' song; Woman's Worth, playing in the bedroom. He opened the bedroom door and was shocked with surprise as Sheena laid naked on the king size bed with nothing on but a red bow.

"Just a little house warming gift I thought you might like. T-Money's smile became even brighter as he noticed the table full of delights. There was whipped cream, honey, strawberries and chocolate glaze!

"Come help daddy get undressed." Watching Sheena walkover to him was pure pleasure. At 5 feet 8 inches tall, Sheena was a sight for sore eyes. She had nice perky full breasts with nipples as dark as the midnight. Her pussy hair was shaved in a nice U-shape with thighs that seem to call his name every time she took a step. She also had some of the prettiest feet T-Money had ever laid eyes on.

"You like what you see, daddy?"

"Damn straight!"

"Well show me how much you miss me." T-Money dropped down on his knees, placed one of Sheena's legs across his shoulder and slowly started kissing the inside of her thigh.

"Ooh daddy, don't tease me." T-Money kept going until she wanted to collapse on the floor. Sheena then laid back at the foot of the bed and spread her legs wide open.

"You want a taste, daddy?"

"But of course."

"Then come and get it!" When T-Money got closer she took her index finger and slid it in her wet pussy and then pulled it out and stuck it in T-Money's mouth.

"Ooh yeah baby, suck it. Suck all my juice off my finger." After a few moments, T-Money stood up and released his full erection right in front of Sheena.

"Damn baby, is all that for little ole me?"

"To do with as you please." Sheena then started licking on the head of his dick while playing with his nuts.

"Aww yeah, baby girl. Make daddy cum." Sheena relaxed her throat and started deep throating the length of his shaft.

"Ooh shit, baby. That feels so good. Slurp on that dick, baby girl. Slurp it."

As Sheena started going faster, T-Money started losing control. "Oh fuck baby, I'm gonna cum. I'm cumming." As T-Money released his load, Sheena didn't let one drop hit the floor.

"Damn, baby! What you trying to do? Lock a nigga down?"

"Only if you're ready because trust me, I'm not going nowhere."

On the other side of town, Ratt was putting his plan together. "Okay, y'all know what to do. As soon as you see anyone of these cats, I want to be the first one to know." Ratt had put together a little team of smokers because he knew the power of crack was far stronger than the will of most men. And just as sure as one of them seen Strapp, T-Money or Young World, he knew they would call him.

Young World had just landed in the Bahamas and getting off the plane, he spotted his Bahamian princess. "Hey Sweetheart."

"Don't hey sweetheart me. Give me a hug." After hugging Sheila for what seemed like hours the two of them headed off for what would definitely be a relaxing night.

Strapp meanwhile was back on the grind putting together a plan of his own. He had huddled up over fifty smokers to help put his plan in action. "Now listen, I know all of y'all love to get high and I can promise not one but all of y'all a high for a long time to work with me."

"What do you want us to do, Strapp?"

"Yeah, we like to get high but you and T-Money always look out for us."

"Well, here's what I need. I need to know the first person who comes asking y'all about me or T-Money. I'm also interested if he asks about somebody named Young World. You will know it's strange because the person or persons asking won't be from around this area. Just tell them you'll keep your eyes open and to give a way to get in touch with them."

"That's it, Strapp?"

"Yep, that's it. I have a fifty piece for all of y'all so come on and get it." Strapp knew one thing for sure, sooner or later, Ratt would come looking and since he isn't from around here he would have to ask smokers because asking another hustler could get him killed in the hood and besides most smokers don't have any morals.

CHAPTER 9

"Ooh yeah, Sheila, suck that dick good for Young World." Sheila had Young World on the verge of breaking down but decided to prolong the excitement.

"Tell me who dick this is! This me." With his balls in her mouth, Young World was fighting a losing battle so he gave in.

"It's your dick, baby. It's your dick."

"Then make me know it." Sheila then laid on her back and hooked both legs behind her neck.

"Show me it's my dick!" Young World had a different plan as he gently kissed Sheila right on her pussy.

"Ooh baby, that's it! Eat this pussy." Young World slowly circled her clit with his tongue sending her body into a frenzy of convulsions.

"Oh shit World, I'm cumming. I'm cumming right in your mouth, babbyyyyy. I can't, I can't, I can't take it baby." Sheila tried to pull away but Young World's grip was too strong as she lost all control. After hours of lovemaking, Sheila noticed the stress that was within Young World and gave him her ear to listen.

"What's wrong baby?"

"It's just a lot going on in my life and I'm trying to grasp everything at one time."

"Is there anything I can do to help?"

"Trust me baby, you're doing more than enough."

"I don't know why Tiesa had to bring our past to the present. She had to know there was a better way of dealing with that than bringing it to this. I hope no one else had any idea of their own. But as long as it's not T-Money then I could care less. So what if I took a little pussy! She should have thanked me for preparing her for the world. But now that's one less problem I have to worry about. I'll just drop the numbers on the next package to take their minds off it!"

"Agent Harris, we got the name of the person at the address you requested, Tiesa Farlin."

"Okay. Thank you very much. Agent Smith, did you hear that?"

"Sure did! Seems like Tiesa and our gunshot victim that died has the same name."

"Yeah, Linny Farlin and Tiesa Farlin. And both are native of Jamaica. I say we run that name through our international investigation and see what we come up with."

"That's a good idea. Let's get to it."

"Alright and we'll meet back up for lunch."

It had been six weeks since all of the killing and T-Money and Sheena had become quite the item. He had tested her on several occasions to see if it was about the money but she passed every time with flying colors. He even had her carry his guns through the airport check point. Even though he had paid the guards to let her through, she did it with no hesitation because he said it would be alright. She never had any questions. She cooked. She cleaned. And most of all she did everything she could to make him happy. In just a short period of time T-Money had fallen in love! Sheena had earned what it took most a lifetime to achieve…trust. When they made love it was always different and most of all it was great. Yes T-Money couldn't see being without her and tonight he would show her. He had made arrangements at a fancy nightclub called Premier just for the two of them. He had been out and brought a 7 carat yellow diamond and tonight was the night.

"Baby girl, don't forget we have reservations tonight at 8 p.m. So be ready when I come back."

"Okay, baby you going into town?"

"Yeah, I have a few errands to take care of."

"Okay. I'll see you tonight."

Back across town everything was quiet on the strip until an all-black mustang pulled up.

"You looking to get high, buddy?"

"Nah, then keep it moving."

"I will but let me ask you a question."

"What do I look like 411?"

"No but I will make it worth your while."

"How much we talking?"

"$100 and maybe more if you can be more helpful."

"Okay what do you want to know?"

"I'm looking for T-Money or Strapp. Can you help me?"

"I haven't seen T-Money but I seen Strapp yesterday on Martin Luther King at the park."

"Is he there now?"

"I doubt it because it's not dark enough."

"Oh, he only comes out at night?"

"Yeah, because it's hard to be seen on camera and that's how he works."

"Where else does he be at?"

"This $100 ain't gonna be enough."

"You trying to get rich?"

"I might as well because I could die trying."

"That's fair. Here's another $100."

"Well, sometimes he at this girl's house named "B" over on Ft. King."

"How many people stay there?"

"Just her."

"What color is the house?"

"It's green and tan."

"Alright. Well I appreciate it. What's your name?"

"Everybody just calls me Red."

"Okay Red, maybe I'll be back."

"As long as you bring C.O.D., you alright with me."

"Oh every time, Red, every time!" Red didn't know it but in actuality he had just signed his death certificate. Because one thing that's for sure is that in the hood, the streets have eyes and even the walls can talk.

"Ooh yeah, Strapp, this is your pussy!"

"Whose pussy?"

"Yours Strapp. It's yours babbbbbyyyy."

"You like that?"

"Ooh yes baby."

"Come here and let B suck that dick."

"Beg, bitch! Make me know you want to suck it."

"Plleeeasseee baby, let me suck that big long black dick." Strapp then pulled his dick out and watched B go to work like a woodpecker on wood. "Ooh yeah, that's it baby. Take all that dick. Take it all." Roof, roof, roof. "Strapp, you brought that dog again?"

"Get up bitch! Get up!"

"What's wrong, baby?"

"Killer doesn't like people he doesn't know."

"And?"

"And that means you got somebody in your yard."

"Hey, you sure this is the house?"

"Yeah. Why?"

"Ratt didn't say anything about a dog."

"Man, fuck that dog. We got a job to do so let's do it."

Strapp knew his dog so he knew there was somebody in the yard, which now gave him the advantage because he now was looking at two people dressed in all black creeping by the bedroom window.

"Listen B, I want you to get at the foot of the bed and fake like I'm putting that dick on ya.

"What you want me to say?"

"Bitch, do what you been doing. You know a nigga can't hurt that pussy anyway."

"Yes, I have a reservation for two at 8."

"Oh yes Mr. and Mrs. Hampton, I presume?"

"Yes."

"Right this way."

"Mrs. Hampton, huh?"

"You like it?"

"Yeah I like it! Too bad it ain't for real."

"Well one day we'll have to see what we can do about that."

"I hear you baby, I hear you."

"Can I get y'all something to drink while you're waiting to order?"

"Yes, I'll have whatever she's having."

"Baby, you know I'm having a real drink and you don't drink."

"Well tonight, I feel like a change."

"Okay baby, if you say so."

"Ooh yeah, Strapp, get this pussy, baby. Get it."

"Hey come on man, I hear them in this room." As the two masked men were creeping up to the bedroom window, Strapp was creeping up behind them.

"Ooh yes, I'm cumming baby. I'm cumming."

"Damn dawg. This nigga on some real quiet type shit because I ain't heard this nigga say nothing!"

"That's because I'm right here!" Boom, boom, boom, pop, boom! When they heard Strapp behind them it was too late. Three shots from his pistol grip pump left a hole and a bloody mess on the back of the house.

"Baby, you alright?"

"Yeah, I'm straight. The nigga just tried to get a shot off."

"You know somebody gonna call the police."

"Don't panic! Just go sit on the front porch and when they do come by this way if they ask you about the shots just tell them somebody was shooting out the window of a car."

"Okay."

After dinner, T-Money excused himself from the table and was gone for about twenty minutes. "Where the hell did he go?" Right then all the lights went off. "What the hell!" The next thing that was seen was a lit up sign with 'Sheena, will you marry me' on it. And then Ribbon in the Sky came over the intercom. Sheena was lost for words as tears started coming down her face at a rapid pace.

"Sheena, all my life, I've been searching for happiness to make me complete. And being with you makes me happier than I've been in a long time. The Bible tells me to seek and you shall find and my mother always says that good things come to those who wait. And I just want you to know that I've finally found what I've been looking for and it would give me great pleasure if you would be my wife!"

At that moment, Sheena was in pure shock. She was surrounded by applause and her heart was beating fast. "I do, I mean I will." And then she ran and jumped in T-Money's awaiting arms.

"I love you, Mr. Hampton."

"I love you, too, Mrs. Hampton!"

The police had come and left with few questions being that this was a black neighborhood a shooting wasn't really a top priority. Strapp had cleaned up the mess and told B that he would have the hole fixed tomorrow.

"Where you going, baby?"

"First, I'm going to drop these bodies off so they'll be found."

"Why?"

"So whoever sent them will know that the job ain't been done. And then I'm going to find out how they knew where I was at."

"What you want me to do?"

"Get a few things together and get a room. And then tomorrow find somewhere else to stay on the outskirts of town and then call me."

"So when is the next time I'm going to see you, Young World?"

"You know honestly, Sheila, I can't say. It could be tomorrow. It could be next year but with me best believe that even when you ain't with me you're with me. That's why I'm glad you're over here because in a dirty world surrounded by a dirty game you're the only pure thing I have!" Sheila being determined not to lose what she had knew just what she had to do. She had been thinking about it for a while but now it was clear to her that this was the man for her. And to have him she was prepared to go against tradition.

CHAPTER 10

"Hey Ratt, look at this. We were wondering why we didn't hear from the twins and this is why." They were looking at the morning paper which was headlined: Two Slain Executioner Style. Two bodies found right in front of Ocala Police Department with a note that read 'If you want something done right then do it yourself'. "Fuck man, this is harder than I thought."

"But one way or another they're going down!"

"Check and see if our other connect got something on T-Money. These niggas got to die."

"Hey Strapp, where you been?"

"Let me ask the motherfucking questions! You got something for me?"

"My bad Strapp, there was this black Mustang that came by here about two nights ago. They didn't buy nothing they just stopped and talked to Red."

"Oh yeah. Is that the only person they talked to?"

"Yep. And they gave him $200."

"Okay here. That's a whole eight ball don't kill yourself. Oh, one more thing."

"What's up?"

"Where is Red at now?"

"He's down there by the projects."

"Alright, be easy. Oh, one more thing. If that car comes back around here get a number or tag number or something."

"I got you, Strapp."

It's a goddamn shame how a smoker will sell their soul for something that's not long lasting. But life is all about choices and the choice Red made was death!

"Agent Smith, what do we have?"

"Well for starters, the shooting victim Linny Farlin and the missing Tiesa Farlin are related but it gets better."

"Oh yeah?"

"Yes, our international investigation shows a Shaman Farlin native of Jamaica under investigation for smuggling large amounts of cocaine in the U.S."

"Seems like we need something more to go on because everything we have is speculation."

"Yeah but even the great criminals make a mistake. We just have to make sure they pay for it."

"Hey Red."

"Yeah Strapp."

"Let me holla at you for a second." Since a smoker's first agenda is to get high he didn't even think about the fatal mistake he made previously.

"Yeah, what's up Strapp?" When Red stuck his head in the window it would be his last mistake. Strapp pulled him by the back of his head and stuck a forty-five magnum in his mouth and pulled the trigger. The tenants of the projects would never give up Strapp to the police because it was he who paid the peoples' light bills. It was also he who the kids loved. It was he who made sure that the people in the projects didn't want for nothing. So to them Red had did something wrong and no one would ever know who did it as they too would forget!

Ring, ring, ring. "Hello."

"What's the deal Money?"

"Young World, I see you finally gave me a call. Where you at?"

"I'm back in town."

"Well shit, we need to meet I got something to tell you."

"That's good because I need to talk to you, too."

"Okay, let's meet at the mall."

"Alright. I'll see you in about ten minutes." T-Money was feeling so good with his soon to be wife at his side. He was thinking about what Young World wanted to talk about and didn't even notice the dark blue Regal that was following him.

"Hey baby girl, you can drop me off at the mall and head on home."

"Alright but tell Young World don't have you out too late because I'm in the mood for a little freaky business."

"Okay but it's my turn to be in control."

"Baby, what do you want to do?"

"I guess you'll just have to wait and see, won't you!"

"So what's this good news you got to tell me?"

"Me and Sheena, we getting married."

"What! You mean to tell me, Mr. Mack himself, is giving up his playa card!"

"I know right. But she's the one, World."

"How do you know?"

"It's the way I feel when I'm with…" Ring, ring, ring. "Hold on World, this is Strapp. What's up with you, Strapp?"

"I need to holla at ya!"

"What's wrong dawg?"

"The nigga Ratt tried to have me took out."

"Where the fuck you at homie?"

"I'm in the projects on the front line."

"Well sit tight, me and World coming over."

"Alright. Peace out."

"What's up, Money? Is Strapp alright?"

"Yeah, but he said Ratt sent somebody to take him out."

"We got to take this nigga out, Money. He ain't from here but he know a few people."

"Oh trust me, as soon as we find out where this nigga lay his head it's a wrap for him. Trust me!"

"Hey Ratt."

"Yeah, what's the low?"

"We followed that bitch ass nigga T-Money to the mall."

"That's good but it's too many people there."

"I know but listen. He had this girl drop him off and we followed her to this big ass house in Marion Oaks."

"Oh yeah."

"You want us to take the bitch out?"

Young World

"Nah, don't do nothing we might finally have our advantage. Just stay on post and let me know if that nigga comes there."

"Bet that up."

"Strapp, what's the deal homie."

"Just another day in the hood."

"You good though?"

"Yeah, I'm straight. What's up with you, Young World?"

"Ready to deal with this nigga, Ratt. Where was you at anyway, Strapp?"

"Over my little hood bitch house B on Ft. King."

"Damn, how did he get that type of info?"

"A smoker they call Red."

"Well shit, let's deal with him first!"

"Too late. It's already taken care of."

"That's the one thing about you Strapp; if it need to be dealt with you always handle your B.I."

"That's the only way I know, Young World. But trust me this nigga gonna fuck up and when he does, he can give his soul to the Lord because y'all know what time it is."

"Yeah, his ass belongs to us!"

"Man, since we out we should head to the café tonight."

"I'm gonna kick it with y'all for a little bit but I'm still celebrating."

"Celebrating what, nigga?"

"Oh my bad, Strapp. I forgot to tell you I'm getting married."

"Aww fuck dawg, ya girl got fire like that?"

"Call it what you want to but it is what it is."

"Shit. Do you, playa. I ain't mad at you."

"Shit when all of this shit is over, I might get married, too." Young World said.

"Hell, I might have to walk my hood bitch to the alter, too." They all laughed and headed to get something to eat. Back at Sheena's house, she was in a good mood. She had accomplished her goal of finding the right man. And now she would do anything in her power to make what they have last a lifetime.

At the Café, the boys were having a good time. They had their Hummers out with the music playing, T.V.'s showing and the girls were hanging out trying to come up.

"I'm glad I let y'all talk me in to hanging out tonight."

"You might as well have a little fun before you tie the knot."

"Damn Money! What really made you come to that?" Strapp asked.

"I'm comfortable with her dawg. She's everything I need and want in my woman."

"Did you put her through our test?"

"No doubt! I left $300,000 like it hadn't been counted or nothing, just laying around and not only did she not take nothing, she counted it and put it in stacks."

"Man, y'all niggas on some Bonnie and Clyde type shit." Young World said.

"Trust me, Young World, if a girl is about money it will show. Tell me what thief do you know that won't steal? What killer you know that won't kill? The next time you go see your girl tell her you lost everything and that you don't have nothing and see what happens. Most will stick around for a while because they know if you're a hustler, you'll come up again. Real people hold on because they know in life there's bitter and sweet. Nothing stays sweet unless it's a real effort being made to keep it that way!"

"Damn nigga, you should write a book. That's some heavy shit."

"Yeah but the game is to be told not sold."

"I thought it was the other way around?"

"It is for the average nigga because he doesn't know any better. See if you sell it then everybody can have it but if you tell it then you can choose who you tell it to."

"Hey Bigg, ain't that the nigga you said tried you because he had his guns and you didn't?"

"Yeah, that's that pussy nigga!"

"Well, let's straighten this shit out."

"Hey Money, look at your 2:00. Ain't that the nigga Bigg headed this way?"

"Yeah, that's him."

"We got a problem Money?" Young World asked.

"I'm straight. Just watch the dude that's with him. He's a powder head and he might be high."

"Oh don't worry about nothing, Money. I got him!"

"What's up, fuck nigga! Ain't so tough without your guns, huh tough guy?" At that point, Strapp and Young World pulled out their heat.

"Now why would he need his when we got ours?" Young World said.

"Hey powder head, go ahead and reach for your gun so I can bust a nut." Strapp said.

"Always need your guns but one day you won't have them."

"Now see that's where you're wrong! I don't need no guns. As a matter of fact, we can settle this shit right now!" As T-Money's voice grew louder so did the crowd.

"Hey man, what's going on?"

"I think T-Money and that big dude are going to fight."

"Aww man, big as that dude is, T-Money better shoot that nigga."

"You must don't know!"

"Know what?"

"That nigga T-Money is nice with his hands."

"He better be or he's going to get beat the fuck down."

"Nah dude, that can't happen anyway. Don't you see that nigga Strapp right there? He will kill a nigga and don't even think about it."

"So what you trying to do, Bigg?"

"Oh, you want to fight me?"

"Well, I ain't trying to dance with you."

"Ooh, ooh, ooh."

"Man, y'all shut the fuck up!"

"Let's do it then."

"Hey Ratt, ain't that your dude right there?"

"Right where?"

"Getting ready to fight that big nigga."

"Yeah that's that nigga. We might not have to worry about him but get a little closer just in case."

Bigg charged T-Money but was too slow as T-Money side stepped him and delivered a two punch combination to the side of his head. Thump, thump. Being as big as he was put him at a disadvantage especially because he couldn't grab T-Money.

"That's the best you got, big boy?" Bigg swung again grazing T-Money's lip. Not landing solid would prove bad for Bigg. T-Money hit him with two rights followed by a punch in the throat which dropped Bigg straight to the floor.

"Damn, ole boy pretty good with his hands, Ratt."

"Yeah but put a couple of them bullets in him and see what time it is then." Right as T-Money got ready to him with another combination a flurry of bullets rang out. Pop, pop, pop, pop, pop, pop, pop, pop. When Strapp and Young World seen where the shooting was coming from they too opened up fire. Boom, boom, boom, pop, pop, boom, pop, pop. After several minutes of gunfire the shooting stopped.

"Hey Money, are you okay?"

"Yeah, I'm good. Strapp, you alright?"

"Yeah, we all cool but that nigga got lost quick."

"Yeah but he's going to have to be dealt with tonight so let's bounce."

"Nigga, why didn't you bust your gun on them niggas?"

"Oh I guess you didn't see that them cats beat me to the punch."

"Them niggas wasn't going to shoot."

"Man, I heard about that dude Strapp and he ain't nothing nice."

"What you pulling his dick now!"

"I'm just keeping it real."

"You better be lucky them other cats went to shooting because dude was kicking your ass."

"Man, shut up and take me to the crib."

"Damn! Can you shoot?"

"It was too many people to get a clear shot."

"Yeah, but you didn't hit shit!"

"Don't worry, we will get them cats. Trust me."

"Agent Smith, we just got reports of a shooting down at the Café."

"Well okay, what are we waiting for? Let's go."

"Ooh yeah, Pimp, get this pussy!"

"You like that?"

"Ooh yeah baby, that feels so good. Fuck me harder. Harder baby, harder!"

"Damn Money, sounds like we don't have to worry about the nigga, Pimping Slim, because he getting his rock off."

"Yeah, sounds like the nigga handling his B.I. Ssshhh, ssshhh. I can hear that nigga Bigg running his mouth."

"Yeah, it's coming from that room over there!"

"Oh, don't even trip Bigg, because as soon as we catch up with them niggas again, it's over for them."

"You damn right! Because as soon as I see him I'm putting some hot lead in his ass. No questions asked. And then I'm going to find that bitch Sheena and kill her ass, too. But only after I fuck her first." Hearing Bigg talk about the woman that he now loved drove T-Money to the point of no return.

"When we go in boss hit that nigga that's with Bigg first and then I'll kill that nigga."

"Ooh, that's it Pimping. I'm cumming. I'm cummng!"

BOOM!

"What the fuck!"

Strapp had kicked the door in and he, Young World and T-Money was thrown back for a minute as the guy that was with Bigg earlier was positioning himself to suck Bigg's dick.

"Well, well, well. What do we have here?" With Bigg and his friend being caught off guard it was nothing he could do.

"Money, this why he didn't realize what he had with ole girl because he a motherfucking bitch his damn self." Fuck you was the last words he would get out his mouth as T-Money began pumping hollow tips in their bodies.

"Pimping, those were shots. Baby, I'm scared."

"Don't worry. Just stay here and if you hear any more shots then call the police."

Pimping Slim eased down the hallway only to be met with a face full of steel.

"Whoa, whoa, whoa. Please don't kill me man."

"Please, nigga, shut the fuck up." Young World said. Pimping Slim was so scared that he forgot he had a gun, too.

"And drop that gun before I blast that ass!"

"Strapp man, help me out man. You know I won't say shit."

"Oh I know but it ain't my call."

"Listen!" T-Money said. "I ain't gonna kill you but you know how the game goes. If I hear of or even think you said something to anybody including that bitch you got in there, you're a dead ass and the world ain't big enough for you to hide. You understand?"

"Hey man, I don't even get down like that."

"Well for your sake you better hope not. Oh and you need to get somebody to clean that mess up and the next time you hire a bodyguard make sure the nigga ain't no punk. The way they are is the way I found them."

"Don't even worry about it, I'll handle it myself."

"In that case, holla at me when you ready to cop some more dope." When they left Pimping Slim went in the room and seen exactly what T-Money was talking about. "Goddamn punk! Around here with muscles popping out his ears and all he wants to do is strong arm some ass. I'm glad he's dead, punk motherfucker!"

"Y'all think it's cool that we left that nigga alive?"

"Oh trust me, he ain't a dumb nigga."

"And besides dudes like him can't afford to be away from their lifestyle so in the end he knows he made a bad business investment."

"Always remember this, Young World. What the game don't teach you, you'll learn the hard way but the hard way may not give you a chance to learn! So getting a second chance in the game is like getting another life with a little more knowledge."

"Well Agent Harris, did anybody see anything?"

"As a matter of fact they did. Turns out that our T-Money had a fist fight but he wasn't the one shooting. But seems like the shooter could have been shooting at him or the person he was fighting."

"Well I tell you what. Let's try to find out who the other guy was."

"Good idea."

"Fellas, let's get together tomorrow and try to get a play on Ratt."

"Yeah because I'm willing to bet that was him or somebody on his team that was doing the shooting."

"Well if that's the case then we need to handle this as soon as possible because I have a wedding to plan. As a matter of fact, I'm heading home to my beautiful soon to be wife now so, I'll see y'all tomorrow."

CHAPTER 11

Sheila was just arriving in Ocala. She had booked the first flight she could get and with passion in her eyes and love in her heart she was headed to try and secure the only man she truly loved. "I wonder if those guys can help me find Young World? I'll just pull over and ask them. I need some gas anyway."

Ratt and his sidekick had pulled over to make a call from the pay phone. "Oh shit!"

"What's up dawg?"

"Man, look at this fine motherfucker right there."

"She must be new around here because I've never seen her."

"Well evidently she knows you because she's headed over this way."

"Excuse me; I was wondering if y'all could help me out."

"And how may I be of service to you, ma?"

"I was looking for a real good friend of mine but I'm not from here and he doesn't know I'm in town."

"Well, what's this lucky fella's name?"

"Y'all might know him by Young World." When Ratt heard Young World's name he knew instantly that this was his ace in the hole. "That name sounds familiar but let me make a few calls while you get your gas."

"Okay."

"I'll be right back."

"Ratt, she can't be talking about that bitch ass nigga that we looking for!"

"The one and only."

"Well, what are we going to do?"

"I plan on sending a message. And a deadly one at that!"

"Did you have any luck?"

"Yeah, we found him."

"Can you guys show me where he's at?"

"Sure, just follow us." As Sheila got in her car she was so caught up in seeing Young World that she didn't realized the danger she put herself in.

"I finally get the chance to show him that I'm for real about our love and I want it to last forever." If only Sheila had any idea she would turn around and be gone. Since she didn't, her life and his world would never be the same.

Ring, ring, ring. "Hello, Hampton's residence."

"What you doing, baby girl?"

"I'm waiting on you."

"Well, do what you need to do. I'm on the way home."

"Don't take too long, your food might get cold."

"Shit baby, what I like to eat can't never get cold!"

"Ooh baby, you so nasty."

"Would you have me any other way?"

"Hell no baby, hell no!"

Meanwhile across town, Ratt and his partner Boo had led Sheila to one of Boo's townhouses. "Is this it?"

"Yeah. He said when you get here to come on in."

"Well, I sure appreciate your help."

"Oh don't worry about it. He would have done the same thing for me." When Sheila opened the door, Ratt pushed her in the house.

"What's going on?"

"Shut up, bitch!" Whop, whop. Ratt slapped her so hard that she fell down to the floor.

"Boo, tie that bitch up! We gonna have a little fun before we send that message by her."

"Well Agent Smith, we got the name of the guy who was fighting T-Money. His name is Darrell Benson AKA Bigg."

"I wonder why they call him that, Agent Harris."

"Well from my understanding, he's a big fella. But I also heard he has a fetish for getting his dick sucked."

"Hell, Agent Harris, what man doesn't?"

"Yeah, but he doesn't have a preference whether it's male or female!"

"Man, you got to be kidding me. You mean to tell me we're dealing with a goddamn homo thug?"

"Looks that way."

"Well do we have an address on him?"

"Yeah."

"Let's pay him a visit."

Ring, ring, ring, ring, ring. "What!"

"Hey man, you told us to let you know when that nigga got here and he's here."

"Well, y'all sit tight; we'll be there in about 40 minutes."

"Now bitch, take this motherfucking dick!" Boo and Ratt had tied Sheila to the bed and was raping her.

"No, noooo, nooooo."

"Shut up, bitch!"

"Hey Ratt, I'm gonna spread her ass cheeks and you fuck that bitch up the ass."

"Please let me go. Please..."

"Oh don't worry baby, this won't hurt a bit." At that point, Ratt rammed his dick right in her ass. The pain became so intense that she passed out. "Hey man, I think you killed her."

"Ah, ah, I'm cumming. Oh yeah bitch, that's what I call a dead fuck!"

"Man, you sick as fuck man."

"Yeah, I know." Ratt said as he finished jacking his cum over her ass. "Now kill that bitch and let's go!" After Boo put two bullets in her head, they loaded her up and dumped her body in the parking lot of the mall. This would ensure that Young World would come out in the open.

Tears of a Gangster

As T-Money was coming down the street he noticed that there was a dark blue or black Regal at his neighbor's house. Now this wouldn't have been strange except for the fact that his neighbors, the Poole's, were in their late 70's. And being that he had been coming out to the house for a while, it gave him a strange feeling.

"Baby, is that you?"

"Yeah, where are you at?"

"I'm waiting on you upstairs."

"I need you to come here."

"But baby, I got a surprise for you."

"Just come here, damn it!" When Sheena came in the front room, T-money had to admit to himself that Sheena was definitely a sight for sore eyes. And if it wasn't for the fact this blue Regal was out of place he would surely be enjoying himself.

"What's wrong, baby?"

"Come here. Do you see that dark colored car right there?"

"Yeah."

"Well was it there when you was coming home?"

"No baby."

"Are you sure?"

"I'm positive. You know you told me to always be aware of my surroundings and that car wasn't there."

"Okay. Well listen, go put some clothes on and get your heat." As T-Money was watching the unknown car he saw another car and a minivan pull up. "I better call Strapp and Young World."

Ring, ring, ring, ring, ring, ring. "Yeah you've reached that nigga. If it's my nigga then hit me on my hip. If it's anybody else leave a message. Beep."

"Hey man, it's Money. If you get this message I need you and World to come to Marion Oaks, ASAP! Beep."

"Out of all the nights, he picks this night to get his freak on."

"Alright baby, I'm ready." When T-Money turned around Sheena was standing there with all black jeans and an all-black T-shirt with her 380 in her hand.

"I tried to call Strapp and World but I got no answer."

"Do we need them boo?"

"Well it looks like whoever it is has reinforcements."

"Well I'm with you baby and it's whatever!" T-Money knew she was serious but he also knew this looked like it might get hectic.

"Oh shit baby, look!" Sheena said. When T-Money looked out the window he saw about twenty-five guys standing outside the van all with guns!

"Damn Strapp, this party is live as fuck!"

"I told you it was going to be hot."

"Let's step outside for a minute to get some air." Outside the club, Young World noticed the red light on Strapp's phone.

"Looks like you got a call my nigga."

"Yeah somebody left me a message. Might be one of them hoes we seen earlier."

"Yeah them hoes was fine as hell! Well check and see if them hoes trying to do something."

"You damn right."

"You have one message: Hey man, if you get this message, I need you and World to come to Marion Oaks, ASAP! Beep."

"Oh fuck World, let's roll!"

"Alright, y'all know what the deal is. When we get up close y'all let loose and then we going in to make sure they're dead! Y'all know the police will be coming soon so let's do this shit and be out."

"Sheena, listen. Go downstairs and go to the jet skis. When you get there call Strapp's phone and tell him to meet us at the intersection at the bridge on 75. Now go!"

"What about you, baby?"

"I'm going to get this money and meet you down there. Now go!" Reluctantly, Sheena did as she was told. She didn't want to leave her man but she knew he knew what he was doing. Upstairs, T-Money was opening the safe to grab the money that he kept in a duffel bag when the gunshots started.

Ring, ring, ring. "Yeah!"

"Strapp, they shooting at us."

"Who is this?"

"This is Sheena!"

"Well, just stay calm. Where is Money?"

"He's upstairs getting the money. He said meet us at the intersection by the bridge on 75."

"Man, fuck the bridge I'm coming to get y'all."

"No Strapp, it's too many of them. Just meet us at the bridge."

"Alright, we're on the way."

Upstairs, T-Money had grabbed the money and was waiting on the shooting to stop. He knew that they were trying to eliminate the chance of a surprise so they were taking no chances. As soon as the shooting stopped he stared running downstairs.

"Okay, y'all know what time it is. Ratt wants both of them dead so let's make it happen."

"Agent Smith, there's been a report of repeated gunshots out in Marion Oaks."

"We got an address?"

"Yeah."

"Well, let's get going."

"You think they made it, Strapp?"

"I don't know, World. I should have just went on out there like I started to. I tell you what World, when we catch up with Ratt, he's one dead ass!"

"Listen."

"What is that?"

"Sounds like jet skis."

"There they go right there."

As T-Money and Sheena came around the bend, he could see Strapp and Young World waiting.

"There they go right there, baby." As they pulled up to the bank, Strapp and Young World came running.

"Hey man, y'all alright?"

"Yeah dawg, you know how I do it."

Tears of a Gangster

"Man, what the fuck happened?"

"On my way home I recognized a blue or black Regal that seemed out of place. So when I went to get Sheena to confirm it and come back there was a small army out there. So that's why I said don't come."

"Well, what you wanna do?"

"Let's get a room and we'll figure it out in the morning."

"Well, let's be out."

"Hey Ratt, my boys say that they got away."

"Got away! Got away how?"

"He had a passage in the basement that leads to the lake out back."

"Hold up."

"What's wrong?"

"I hear the police. Alright boys let's get ghost."

"I'll call you guys later on."

"What's up with our bread?"

"It's already in your van."

"In that case, hit us up if you need us."

Arriving on the scene, Agents Smith and Harris were in disbelief the house that stood before them was in ruins. Bullet holes were everywhere. Big chunks of the house had been knocked out.

"Man, what came here, a small army?"

"I don't know but if anybody was in there they didn't survive this."

"Well, let's find out." When they reached the front door to open it, the door just fell in.

"Whoever did this meant business."

"Man, look at this house. Somebody was living in luxury to the fullest."

"Do we have a name for the owner of the house?"

"Nothing's showing up, sir."

"What do you mean nothing is showing up?"

"Well apparently the house is in the name of Jane Doe."

"You mean to tell me that in this day and age that you can get a house fully furnished with utilities and all under a fake pretense!"

"That's what it looks like, sir."

"Agents, y'all might want to take a look at this up here." When the agents got upstairs they were looking at two state of the art safes.

"Whoever lived here, they have or had money to burn."

"Hey y'all look down here." When they got downstairs the shocking events continued as they found a secret passage that lead to the lake out back. Disgusted the agent yelled in rage.

"I want this whole house fingerprinted and tore up from the floor up. If the owners have a problem then they'll contact us. Now get busy!"

The next morning Strapp, Young World, Sheena and T- Money all sat at the breakfast table in the hotel lobby replaying the events of yesterday in their heads. "We all know that this was Ratt's work. We need to check all of our connects and see if we have anything on this cat."

Sheena

"Hold up y'all. Here comes a special news flash. "We interrupt this program to bring today's breaking news. At 6:30 a.m. this morning, the body of Sheila Matise was found in the Paddock Mall parking lot in what looks to be a gang style slaying . The victim was found with two gunshot wounds to the head. This is News Channel 6 with breaking news hour on the hours. Stay tuned for more at 12:00 noon."

When everybody turned around nobody could mistake the pain and hurt that was going on in Young World as tears rolled down his face at a rapid pace.

"Nah baby boy, don't tell me it was kinfolks."

"That was my girl, dawg!"

"Damn, I'm sorry dawg." Strapp said.

"I left her in the Bahamas. I don't even know what she was doing over here."

Beep, beep, beep. "We interrupt this program to bring you this special bullctin. As reported earlier the body of Sheila Matise was found in the Paddock mall parking lot at 6:30 a.m. It has also been learned that the victim was carrying a man's wedding ring with the inscription that reads 'I love you, Young World'. Stay tuned for more breaking new from News Channel 6."

By now Young World was boiling uncontrollably.

"Man, Young World, I can't know how you feel but my heart goes out to you and her family. If there's anything I can do just say it and it's done!"

"Just let me talk to you alone for a minute."

"Okay, y'all heard him, leave us alone for a minute."

"Okay, Money. We'll be right over here. Stay strong, Young World."

"Money, what am I supposed to do now? I loved that girl with all I am."

"You just got to be strong and hold on. I'm not a saint or nothing but I know that God says he'll never put more on you than you can bear!"

"I was going to ask you to be my best man after I told you I was going to get married. But now I don't have the one I love and I don't know what to do."

"Let me be frank if I can. I feel your pain because I love you like a brother but right now we need to get a drop on this mothafucking Ratt and blow his ass away!"

"Look at me, dawg. I'm all crying and shit."

"Word to the wise, my young brother. In this cruel life we live in that's full of pain and hurt and I'll be the one to tell you that at some point and time, even gangsters cry."

CHAPTER 12

"Man, how the fuck did they get away from all that firepower?"

"I don't know but I'm starting to believe this nigga T-Money is some kin to a cat."

"What you talking about, Ratt?"

"I mean this nigga must have nine lives!"

"Well, what's our next move?"

"I don't know yet but we'll figure it out in the morning. As a matter of fact, send out a few of the boys and see what they can come up with."

T-Money didn't want Young World to make an emotional mistake while they were trying to get a play on Ratt, so he checked Sheena and Young World in at the motel.

"Strapp, we got to take care of this nigga Ratt!"

"Yeah my boy D-Lo told me to come thru he had a dime that needed to be dropped."

"Well let's go holla at him."

"We will but before we go anywhere I need to holla at you."

"What's up homie?"

"Man, I been thinking and we seriously need to get out of this game."

"And why is that?" T-Money asked.

"Man, over the last few days these losses have been too close to home. And besides look at you in love and shit!"

"Man, look the fuck out."

"Nah, for real Money. And besides I got a little hood bitch that I'm feeling myself."

"Alright then, let's make a deal! We kill this nigga Ratt, first. Give the game 60 days and get the fuck out."

"I'm with that."

"Then it's settled."

"D-Lo, what's the deal homie?"

"What's good with you, Strapp and Money?"

"What you got for us?"

"It's some new cats over in the Quarters and one of them is driving a dark blue Regal."

"Oh yeah. How many of them is it?"

"I'm not sure but it's at least five of them."

"Good looking, D-Lo. When this shit cools down I got that work for you."

"I appreciate that Money."

"Don't even sweat it."

"So how you want to handle it, Money?"

"I don't want them to even know what hit them but I got a plan to put into effect."

Well you know I'm behind you 100 percent so let's make it happen."

"Man, Ratt the smokers are already waiting to get that early morning high."

"Well listen, let's get this money first and then we can come up with another setup for them bitch ass niggas T-Money, Young World and Strapp." When Ratt opened shop, the smokers were spending mad money.

"Hey Boo, it's a lot of money out here this morning."

"Yeah, I know it's like somebody is giving them money to spend."

"Well I don't care where they get it from just as long as it keeps coming."

"Hey, what do you want to spend?"

"I want to get a fifty but I don't have any money." The woman said.

"Well if you ain't got no money then how you want to get high bitch?"

"I could give you and your boy some head."

"Who is that you talking to Boo?"

"Some trick that wants to give us some head for a hit."

"What she look like?"

"She thick as hell for a smoker. Shit, I'm even thinking about waxing that ass!"

"Well you and Moe hit that ass first and then me, Tony and mark gonna get us a little bit."

As Boo and Moe was taking her in the back room, some more smokers came knocking at the door. "Yeah, what's up?" Tony asked.

"We want $200 worth."

"Okay, y'all wait right there."

As Tony was coming back with the dope he looked up and seen that the three smokers were standing in the house. "I thought I told y'all to wait outside!"

"You did but then I couldn't have gave you this."

"What!" Pop, pop, pop. When Ratt and Mark heard the shots they tried to get up but it was too late as T-Money, Strapp and Young World all stood before them with their guns drawn.

Meanwhile in the backroom, Sheena had tricked Boo and Moe into taking off their clothes leaving their guns in their clothes. That's when she pulled her gun out.

"What the fuck is you doing, bitch!"

"The name's Sheena, you low life hustling muthafucker! And the only way you will ever get a piece of hot pussy will be in hell because that's where you're going!" Pop, pop, pop, pop, pop.

"Man, what the fuck is that?"

"That my friend is the sound of my girl putting in work."

"I knew that bitch was too fine to be a smoker."

"Now get on your knees!" T-Money could see the anger boiling over in Young World so he had to get them tied up and put in the car before things got ugly. After putting Ratt, Tony and Mark in the trunk they drove out to the forest where a white friend of T-Money had a house. He had pit bulls in a cage that seemed to want to bite through the cage to get to the intruders. He also had a swimming pool in the back but the water was dark green.

"Man, I thought we were going to torture these bitch ass niggas!"

"Oh trust me, that's exactly what's going to happen. Get that nigga right there first." Money said referring to Mark. "Now strip naked!"

"What y'all on some gay ass time?" Mark asked trying to be hard.

"Oh you a tough guy, huh?" Whop, whop. Strapp hit him with the butt of his nine.

"Now you going to strip or what?" He got up and did as Money told him.

"Now put him in that empty cage.

"What you up to, Money?" Young World asked.

"I'm about to show them my dark side. You see any nigga can pull the trigger but it takes another type of nigga to do what I'm about to do." T-Money went and grabbed a big bucket and threw the red liquid all over Mark.

"Man, what the fuck is that blood?"

"Exactly!" T-Money then slid the cage with the dogs in it so it was door to door with the cage that Mark was in. "These are what my friend Bill-Bob calls blood dogs. The scent drives them crazy and all they can taste is blood."

"Man Money, you a sick motherfucker." Strapp said.

"Please, please man, don't do it."

"Oh, you ain't so tough no more, huh! Well, it's too late for that begging shit." And with that T-Money let the dogs go. The sight before them was too much for Sheena and Young World as everything they ate for breakfast was now on the ground. One of the Pits went straight for Mark's nuts and shook until his nut sack was no longer a part of Mark's body. The biggest of the Pits went for the kill as he lunged straight for Mark's neck like Mark was another dog. After a few shakes it was over! Mark's body lay limp in the middle of the cage with each one of the dogs eating on a different part.

By now Ratt was begging to get shot. "Man just kill me. Please just pull the fucking trigger, please!"

"Nah playa, you's a bad man, remember! You killed my man's bride to be and I'm going to make sure you suffer for it."

"What's your name, nigga?"

"T-T-Tony."

"What you scared, nigga! You should have thought about that before you thought you was a gangster! Tie this nigga up to that pulley." Strapp being the twisted mind that he is couldn't wait to see what T-Money had up next.

"Hey Money, it's going to be hard to beat that dog shit you did!"

"If you think that was bad wait until you see this."

After Tony was tied up, T-Money lifted him up in the air above the pool.

"What you going to do Money, drown him?" Young World asked. T-Money then lowered Tony down until both his feet were in the water and in a matter of second the water bubbled and his feet were ate through the bone and all could be heard was Tony yelling.

"Oh gggod, oooh god, my feet."

"What the fuck! What is that?" Strapp asked.

"That my friend is a pool of deadly piranhas." By now Ratt was crying. Seeing the cruel death of his two henchmen made reality set in. He had fucked with the wrong nigga!

"You see Young World, as gangster as he is or wants to be just look at his bitch ass cry! Now kill that nigga and let's be out." With that being said, Young World emptied his clip in Ratt's riddled body.

"Let me ask you one question Money."

"What's that World?"

"Why didn't you torture Ratt?"

"I did. The only difference was he suffered a lot more mentally than physically. The anticipation of death is a lot worse than death itself because you know it's coming and there's nothing you can do about it."

CHAPTER 13

Ring, ring, ring. "Hello."

"Everything is back to normal on this end."

"The problem has been dealt with?"

"Yes."

"Are you sure?"

"I'm positive."

"Well okay, let's start the wheels back to spinning."

"That's what I'm talking about."

"How is Young World taking it?"

"I really don't know and can't say. It's not the Ratt situation that's bothering him."

"Well what's wrong?"

"He lost his better half in all this madness!"

"I didn't know he was involved with anybody down there."

"He wasn't! It was his girl from the Bahamas."

"Then that's much worse because he loved that girl."

"I know! And the only reason she was over in the states was because she came to marry him."

"How do you know that?"

"Because when they found her body, they found the ring in her pocketbook with a personal inscription to him."

"Well okay. Y'all go back to normal but keep an eye on him for me please, T-Money!"

"You got my word on that."

"Agent Smith, we have some news."

"Oh yeah, what is it?"

"Well apparently some of the fingerprints found in the house belong to Terry Hampton BKA T-Money."

"How did I figure you were going to say that?"

"But that doesn't make him the villain; it makes him possibly the victim!"

"Are those all the fingerprints that were found?"

"There are some partial prints but whoever they belong to has never been in any trouble therefore, we have no prints to match up."

"Well, have we found out whose name the house is in?"

"Not at this time."

"Keep checking until we come up with something."

After a couple of days things seemed to be back to normal. Uncle Sha had even dropped the price to 9.5 a brick. Young World was trying to keep his mind straight and decided to hit the streets with Strapp instead of playing the laid back role. T-Money, on the other hand, was making his wedding plans with his mother.

"Terry I told you we don't need you! Me and Sheena can do just fine. Besides, the wedding isn't until December anyways. So just leave and let us handle it."

"Okay, okay. I was just trying to help."

"Go help Tony (Strapp) and Jeremy (Young World) do something and leave us be now." T-Money walked out of his mother's house all smiles. He knew deep down in his heart that he was making the right choice. He never knew he would meet the woman of his dreams in the situation that he met Sheena. But true to her word, Sheena was a lady by far and that ride or die bitch that he needed by his side. Mrs. Hampton was thrilled by the idea of her son getting married because she knew this would give him a new outlook on his lifestyle. Just as sure as the wedding was being planned, Mrs. Hampton knew a baby wasn't far behind and if that was the case Terry would definitely need to change his lifestyle!

"Young World, you handling things like you've done this all the time." Strapp said.

"Nah, I ain't never been in the streets but some things come natural. You feel me?"

"Oh no doubt. It's just that we all do things for different reasons. Like me, T-Money told me I didn't have to be in the streets no more because we were on another level now. But I choose the streets because it keeps me on point and this is my comfort zone. Now Money is also from the streets but he's also a great thinker which makes him the perfect person for the position he's in."

"Well me…I'm not sure of my reason but I, too, feel comfortable in the streets." While Strapp and Young World was handling business they had yet to notice the extra eyes that were among the other faces on the block.

"Damn Black, ever since them two came back on the block we ain't making no money."

"Yeah, but what do you expect Carlos? Them niggas are well respected in the hood and besides that, the prices them dudes are working with leave us no choice but to get the leftovers."

"They got prices like that?"

"Hell yeah! Anytime you can sell a quarter kilo for $4500, you better believe you the shit!"

"So what are we supposed to do just up and leave?"

"Hell nah! We just have to come up with a game plan and I think I have an idea."

"Man, fuck a plan. Let's just put some hot lead in them niggas."

"Man, I just told you them dudes are well respected and besides the eyes and ears they have on the street, word is they some cold blooded killers!"

"Shit, I can't tell. Look how they slipping right now."

"Slipping! Man, you couldn't get within 50 feet of them niggas without being gunned down."

"How you figure that?"

"Like I said, I've been observing shit since they came back. You see the extra smokers out there this morning?"

"Yeah, so what."

"Well, they ain't smokers!"

"What do you mean?"

"What I mean is there's a lot of guns out here to hold them niggas down. And see apartments number 19 and 32?"

"Yeah, so what?"

"Look at the windows." At first Carlos couldn't see it but when he focused his eyes, he saw two barrels pointed out each window. "Damn!"

"Yeah, them niggas are on point waiting on some dumb nigga just like you to think they're slipping and get their head bust open."

"Well, what plan do you have?"

"My cousin!"

"What can he do?"

"That's just it. He is a she. My cousin is fine as hell and she ain't new to this. And to top it off, she's not from here so dudes won't even have a clue."

"Well how is she gonna get up under them?"

"All she has to do is get an apartment out here and keep her lifestyle simple. No fancy hairdo's, not too many fly clothes, keep her apartment nice and keep some food in the fridge. We'll get her a used old Honda with tint and after that it's set."

"How is it set?"

"Have you ever seen a top notch nigga without a dime piece? And if you did, better believe he has one on the side."

"Damn Black, you smart as hell!"

"Nah, I just know the game and how it's played!"

"Hey Strapp."

"Yeah. What's up, Skeeter?"

"I know I gets my smoke on but let me holla at ya about something serious."

"Yea, what's up, old playa/"

"Now this what I'm about to tell you ain't a fo-sho thing but just take what I'm saying into consideration. Since y'all been gone it's been two new cats come thru here and put in work."

"And!"

"Well see the thing is since y'all been back they ain't making shit!"

"That's what it's about…making money."

"Yeah but they still coming back every day."

"Well maybe they feel they can make a few dollars before we get here."

"I thought about that so dis morning I went to them to get a little smoke and they said they didn't have nothing. So if you ain't got nothing why come out every day unless you checking something out."

"I feel you, old timer. That's good looking out."

"Yeah, I felt that since you look out for all the people in the projects, it's the least I could do."

"Bet that up, Skeeter!" As soon as the old smoker left, Strapp took notice to the two strangers. He had to admit that the old head was right. There was no reason to be out there if you wasn't gonna get money. But as soon as Young World comes back from the store, he would get to the bottom of it.

Ring, ring, ring. "What's up?"

"Strapp, where are you and Young World at?"

"Man, you know we over here in the projects getting money."

"Well y'all just chill for a minute. I'm coming thru."

"Alright, bet that up."

"Agent Smith, the house is still not coming up under anybody's name but word on the street is that our boys T-Money and Strapp are back in the game. Our informant has even seen Strapp a few times in the projects."

"Has he been able to buy anything from them?"

"Not yet but he said sooner or later."

"Good, because if we can't get them all, then we'll get them one by one."

"You know what they say, don't ya?"

"Nah, what they say?"

"If it will keep my life on track then I'll become a Ratt!"

As soon as T-Money got to the projects he saw Strapp and Young World on the curve.

"What's up with y'all playas?"

"We getting ready to go over here and see what these dudes out here for!"

"Hell, they might be trying to get some money."

"That's just it, we already know they ain't getting no money because they don't have shit but they been out here just taking notice."

"Well in that case, let's go check these niggas out!"

"Sheena, what colors do y'all want to wear in the wedding?"

"I don't know, Mrs. Hampton. I thought maybe you could help me with that."

"First of all baby, you are now a part of this family, so stop calling me Mrs. Hampton!"

"I'm sorry."

"Don't be sorry. Just call me Mama."

"Okay, Mama."

"Well Sheena, that's beautiful."

"Do you think Terry can find a tux to match it?"

"Oh trust me baby, the last thing you have to worry about is him matching you because if I know Terry like I do then he'll go and have one custom made."

"Hey Black, you looking at this shit!"

"Yeah, it looks like them niggas is headed over here."

"Well what are we supposed to do?"

"Just chill Carlos and let me do all the talking."

"Okay but what if they got something else in mind?"

"Then we're shit out of luck!"

As T-Money and his boys got closer T-Money had a bad vibe. "Hey Strapp, stay on point."

"Got ya." But little did T-Money know Strapp had that same feeling.

"Hey Young World." Strapp said. "If anything looks out of place shoot first, ask questions later."

"And you know this homie."

"Hey, what's up with y'all fellas?"

"Ain't nothing. Just chillin." Black said.

"Well, I ain't gonna beat around the bush. Me and my boys want to know what it is y'all want around here."

"No disrespect but the last time I checked it was a free county."

"You know what playa, you right so that's why I'm gonna tell you one time to get the fuck from around here. And the next time we won't be talking because dead men don't talk, ya heard me!"

"You heard what he said, partner? Now beat your feet." Strapp said as he pulled out his brand new 45s."

"Alright home. Just take it easy."

"Trust me, I ain't ya mutherfuckin' homie!"

While driving off Black was completely quiet until Carlos broke the silence.

"Damn Black, you told me to let you do all the talking and then you almost got us killed."

"Man, shut the fuck up! I was trying to figure out who we're dealing with and now I know."

"What do you know?"

"Well for one, we're dealing with three killas."

"How you know that?"

"It's in their eyes but you have to be a killer to see it."

"Hell, I'm a killa!"

"No, you will kill somebody but you're not a killa and there's a big difference! The one who was talking is definitely a killa but he's the calmest of the three. The one they call Strapp now he's a cold blooded killa. If we ever cross paths then there's definitely gonna be a funeral."

"What about the young one?"

"While all the talking was going on he already had his guns out so that lets me know that he's ready for whatever!"

As the weeks went by money was coming in real plentiful. Strapp and Young World had the projects on lock! They never seen Black and Carlos again but Strapp knew that wasn't the end to their run-ins. But while money was being made a new tenant was moving in the projects and word had it that she is fine as hell!

"Hey Strapp, you seen the new girl that moved in the projects?"

"Nah, what's up with her?"

"I don't know because I haven't seen her either but from what I hear she's like that!"

"Well Young World, all I can say is try your pimp hand."

"Oh trust me if she's anything like I hear then it's on. Besides you know what they say. Pimping ain't easy but someone has to do it!"

Ring, ring, ring. "Hello."

"What's up cuz?"

"Hey Black."

"You ready to put this thing in effect?"

"I was born ready, cuz."

"Well, let's get this money!"

"What do I need to do to get at one of them?"

"Trust me all you have to do is walk to the corner store and one of them is bound to get at ya."

"Well alright. I'm gonna head to the store in a minute and I'll get back with you."

CHAPTER 14

"Mama, I got to go to the mall. Do you want to come along?"

"I might as well go and get out this house."

"Well okay. I'm gonna call Terry and let him know where we're going."

"You sure believe in checking in, don't you?"

"It ain't even like that, Mrs. Hampton."

"Child, whatever. I know my son and I know he put that whip appeal on you and got your nose wide open."

"Oooh Mama."

"Oooh Mama, my ass! Come on, let's go. Maybe I'll find somebody to open my nose."

"Okay, make Terry cut up."

"Whatever! I brought him in the world and I'll take him out."

"Ooh, you go girl!"

"What's up, fellas?"

"Nothing much. Money, me and Young World just chillin' out."

"Man, y'all need to give these projects a break and enjoy a little of this money."

"What you got in mind, playa?"

"I'm headed to the mall to spend a little money and then I'll probably go to Gainesville and do the same thing."

"In that case, let us close up shop."

"Hey Skeeter, me and Young World are gone for the day, so we'll holla at you in the morning."

"Y'all gonna leave me hanging?"

"Never that!"

"There's something for you on the back porch of the old house. So be easy."

"Bet that up, Strapp."   As T-Money and the boys were about to pull off something caught T-Money's attention.

"Got-damn it boy, look at this fine mothafucker right here!"

"Oh fuck, that must be the new girl that moved in the projects."

"You mean to tell me that y'all got a fine mothafucker like this in the projects and you haven't said nothing?"

"First of all playa, this is both of our first time seeing her too."

"Yeah Money, it ain't like if she had been staying in the projects that one of us wouldn't have tagged that ass by now. I guess it's gonna have to be Young World because I'm trying to get things right with B!"

"Let me find out you gonna follow me to the altar."

"Well you know what they say; birds of a feather flock together."

"Young World, let me see what you working with."

"Oh no doubt, watch and learn as I show y'all how it's done in my world."

The Goons!

"I sure hope this is one of these guys getting ready to approach me now because I'm tired already of these corner hustlers trying to holla at a diva, like myself, knowing their game ain't up to par."

"Excuse me, lovely lady. How are you doing today?"

"I'm doing just fine.

"Well, I seen you walking this way and was stunned by your beauty so I decided to come give you a compliment in the hopes that I could brighten your day."

"Well thank you and it might turn out to be a good day after all."

"I'm Young World and if you ever want all your days to be better than the next holla at ya boy."

Before Dijuana could respond Young World was headed back to the all-black Mustang that was waiting.

"Damn! That nigga was smooth as hell and on top of that he was fine as a motherfucker. I wonder why they call him Young World. Well I guess in due time, I'll find out because I'm definitely gonna be in touch!"

"Well playa, what's the deal?"

"Oh, it's a done deal. Women always want you to do what's expected so I always do the unexpected."

"You got a point, Young World, but women really get turned on by is mystery! The less they know about you the more attracted they are to you."

"Well, I left it so that if she wants to get to know me better then she'll have to get at me."

"Okay, the ball is in her court so let's see what her next move is."

"If she know like I know, she'll pass me the ball."

As the months passed by things couldn't get better. The wedding was in a couple of days and not only T-Money but Strapp and Young World were also millionaires. But you know what they say, after the calm comes the storm and things often get worse before they get better.

"Damn homie, you finally gonna tie the knot!"

"Yeah Strapp, and the funny thing is it feels right."

"Well, let me be the first to say, I'm happy for you my man. We've been out here in this game for so long and death nor jail hasn't found neither one of us so I guess getting married was a given."

"You know Strapp, I've been thinking and I think this is my last year in the game."

"Well dawg, I tell you what if you can make that six months then I'm out too."

"Why six months and not a year?"

"For one thing, we've already paid up front for the next two shipments. Two, because we all have enough money to last us the rest of our lives provided we do the right thing and make a few investments. Last but not least, the longer we stay in the game the harder it will be to get out."

"Well homie, I guess you'll be getting out too because six months it is."

"Let's try to get Young World to see it our way and if not then he'll be in it by himself."

"Where is he?"

"Knowing him, he's with Dijuana."

"I'm glad he's happy because that might help him make the right decision about the game. What's that look for Strapp? What you thinking?"

"Nothing really but I want you to listen to this theory. Unbelievable fine girl moves in the projects, turns down a few guys who she doesn't know could be big timers and she didn't just move in any projects but the worst projects in town as far as living condition. And to top it all off, she ends up talking to Young World!"

"But from my understanding, he hasn't even tapped that ass yet."

"My point exactly! What girl you know staying in the projects kicking it with one of the towns biggest ballers ain't trying to get her back blown out?"

"Well, why haven't you said anything to him?"

"First of all, it's just a theory. Secondly, the boy's sprung so any negative input from me or anybody else could cause conflict."

"What can we do?"

"Well, I'm gonna go see a friend of mine and see what I can find out."

"Oh, you still kick it with the police girl."

"Got to stay up to par for all of our good. Know what I mean?"

"Well when you find something out, let me know."

"No doubt, playa."

Ring, ring, ring. "Hello."

"What's up, cuz?"

"Ain't nothing Black. Just doing my thing you know."

"Well what are we working with?"

"Right now, I'm keeping about five kilos in the apartment for him and about $50,000. If y'all want that, y'all can just break in and steal that."

"Is that all he'll leave with you?"

"The most I've had is 10 kilos and $100,000 but that was only one time. But why don't y'all just take that because I think I'm gonna stay here instead of going back to Miami."

"Damn cuz, let me find out you done fell for this nigga."

"Nah, it ain't even like that I just think it would be better for me to live being here."

"Well when do you think it's a good time to hit him up."

"Tomorrow would be good because we going to his boy wedding."

"Okay. We will hit it then and then we out."

"Alright cuz, don't even worry about me because I'm straight and this way y'all can leave right after." After hanging up with Dijuana, Black had a bad feeling about his once loyal cousin.

"Hey Carlos."

"Yeah. What's up, Black?"

"Man, that bitch ass cousin of mine is going soft on us dawg."

"She don't want to do it no more?"

"Nah, it's still on but she want us to settle for five kilos and $50,000!"

"Shit, I don't see nothing wrong with that."

"See that's because you ain't looking at the big picture. If he trust her with that then what you think he has at his place?"

"I see what you're saying but if we just kill his ass for what she's talking about then that's alright with me."

"See that's what I'm saying. They ain't even gonna be home."

"So you mean to tell me that this is free money?"

"Yeah. But I'm telling you there's more."

"Man, fuck more. Let's just get this free money and call it a day." Even though Black didn't want to he knew what Carlos was saying was right and if that's all they could get then fine. But if there was any way he could get more then fuck Carlos and his bitch ass cousin! For the right amount, they all could die!

CHAPTER 15

"Well Mama, tomorrow is the day and then I'll officially be a part of the family."

"Girl, whether you get married or not you will always be a part of this family."

"Thank you, Mama."

"Don't thank me yet because we still have to get Terry out of these streets."

"Mama, he said in six more months, it's over."

"Yeah but those will be the longest six months in my life and until there up, I'm still concerned."

"Ooh Mama, don't talk like that because you're scaring me."

"Well, I don't mean to scare you but I've been having a bad feeling for the last couple of weeks. So let's try to cut that six months in half."

"And what if we can't?"

"Then we'll have to do some extra praying!"

Ring, ring, ring. "Yeah, what's up?"

"Hey Money, check this out. Our girl Dijuana Nelson comes from Miami, Florida, 24 years old with one kid named Sondra Nelson."

"I thought our boy said she didn't have any children."

"He did but if he doesn't know this then how can he tell us? But wait there's more. In one of the police reports she was a victim in a home invasion but she lived. But her boyfriend was killed. And this happened on two different occasions. Word on the Miami streets is that's why she left because the brothers of her last boyfriend are looking for her."

"Damn, we need to put Young World up on game."

"Yeah, you're right but we can tell him after the wedding. You just get ready to enjoy yourself."

"Alright, I'll holla at you later."

Meanwhile, Black and Carlos was watching Dijuana apartment in hopes of catching Young World slipping. What they were unaware of was the unmarked police car was also watching Dijuana's apartment.

"Agent Smith, do you think your source is reliable?"

"Yes I do and besides she said that he's not going to deal with nobody hand-to-hand so a sales charge looks like it's out of the question."

"But if we can catch him red handed with the drugs then we can try and prosecute him."

"Don't you think we should get this authorized?"

"We can worry about that after we get him in custody."

Ring, ring, ring. "Hello."

"What's up boo?"

"Oh hey baby. How are you doing today?"

"I'm good but check this out. I'm on my way to your apartment so unlock the door and I'll be there in about five minutes."

"Okay baby. I'll be waiting. Oh and baby, I think tonight would be a perfect night."

"Girl, quit playing. I told you if you're not ready then I can wait."

"Well, the wait is over. Just get here." When Young World hung up the phone, he no longer was thinking about the ten kilos or the $85,000 he had in his duffle bag. Nope, all that was on his mind was finally making love to this beautiful woman of his. He had waited a long time and promised himself that when the time came he would pull out all the stops and tonight was his night! When Young World pulled in front of Dijuana's apartment, he was so busy thinking about making love to Dijuana that all of the street intellect that had been instilled in him was nowhere to be found. So as he stepped out the car with the duffle bag, he was unaware of his surroundings.

"There he is right there, Agent Smith."

"Yeah and it looks like he has just what our girl said he would have."

"There he is, Black. And it looks like we might have hit the jackpot."

"Yeah, well let's do this shit and get it over with."

As Agents Smith and Harris got out the car something caught Agent Harris' attention. "Look, Agent Smith! Looks like our boy is about to get robbed."

"Well, you know we can't have that so let's intercept this."

"Okay, but how are we supposed to do that without giving ourselves away?"

"We can't but with your girl, we will always be able to get another lead on our boy but if he's dead or hurt then it does us no good."

As Young World reached for the doorknob, he heard that all too familiar phrase.

"Fuck nigga, give that money up!"

"Alright playa, just don't shoot."

"Freeze and drop your guns, F.B.I!" Now these wasn't the words that Young World wanted to hear but at that moment nothing sounded better even if it was the boys in blue.

"Drop them right now or we'll shoot!"

"Man, fuck this shit Black, I ain't going to jail."

"Well then you know what to do." It was at that point that all hell broke loose. Pop, pop, bang, bang, bang, boom, boom, boom, bop, bop, boom, pop, pop, pop, bang, bang. During all of this gunfire, Young World managed to get in the apartment.

"Baby, what's going on?"

"I don't know but I ain't staying around to find out. Come on let's get out the back window."

"Black, Black."

"Yeah."

"You alright?"

"I'm hit in the shoulder but I'm straight."

"Well come on, let's get the fuck out of here." They wouldn't know it then but later Black and Carlos would find out that that small war they had created had left two dead agents.

"Man, you think those two agents are dead?"

"I don't know but you need to take me to Gainesville so I can go to the hospital."

"Damn, they fucked us up Black. That was our lick!"

"Yeah, but we would have been sitting in jail right now if it wouldn't have went down the way it did."

"You right and besides that nigga is hot as fuck to have the feds watching him."

"Well after we get this taken care of we will call Dijuana and find out what's what."

"Shit all those bullets that nigga might be dead!"

"I sure hope not, I sure hope not!"

"Baby, what happened back there?"

"Let me think for a minute, boo. There ain't no two ways about it. Those were the feds and some jack boys back there."

"Baby, I'm scared."

"Don't worry, we're gonna get a room and I'm gonna make a few calls."

Meanwhile back in the projects, the police had finally responded to the gunshots. "Bob, what do we have?"

"Well Sergeant, we have two dead white males with gunshots to the torso and head."

"Can we identify them?"

"We're checking their possessions right now. Oh my God Sarg, you might want to look at this."

"Okay, get those reporters back!"

"Aww shit, this is going to get real ugly. We have two dead F.B.I

Agents and no suspects."

"Well, let me make the call while you go door to door and see what you can come up with."

Ring, ring, ring. "Yeah, what's up?"

"Hey World, what the hell is happening in the projects?

"Man, I was just about to call you."

"Why, what's going on?"

"Just meet me at the Hilton on 200 and I'll run it to you."

"Well, give me ten minutes and I'll be there. What room are you in?"

"I'm in room 112."

CHAPTER 16

"Dijuana, turn on the T.V. and see what's on the news."

"Okay."

'We interrupt this program to bring you this breaking news. Tonight Parkhill projects are surrounded with police and federal agents after two federal agents were shot dead in what seems to have been a vicious shoot out. Agents Tom Smith and Danny Harris were killed in the line of duty. That is all we have at the moment but we will keep you posted as more news comes in.'

After hearing that Agent Tom Smith was dead as well as his partner, Dijuana was doing a dance because her violation of the street code could have led to death especially with some of the killers she had messed with. She hated doing it but when she got messed up with that botched home invasion and it left three people dead including a six year old girl, it was either roll with them or get rolled over. But now she found herself in love with someone she really cared for. And now that her contact was dead, she knew that part of her life was over. Now if only she could get her cousin to back off, she could live a normal life. She knew that was her cousin and Carlos who had left the feds dead. Being that they were in town a day earlier gave her the idea that the way they left the feds was the way they were gonna leave her.

Knock, knock, knock. "Get the door, baby. It's probably Strapp."

"Who is it?"

"Strapp."

"Oh hey Strapp. How are you doing?"

"I'm good. Where's Young World at?"

"He's in the bathroom."

"Well, why don't you go to the lobby and get something to eat while I talk to him."

"Alright I'll be back when y'all get finished."

"Man, come on out of there. Did they scare the shit out of you?"

"Ha, ha, ha, very funny."

"Nah, but on the real, what's the deal?"

"All I know is that when I pulled up in front of Dijuana's apartment and got out I heard two phrases. Neither one of them was pleasant. On my right, two niggas in all-black and ski masks told me to give that money up! And on my left, the two F.B.I agents said drop them or we'll shoot."

"And then what happened?"

"I guess some niggas wasn't trying to hear that and started shooting."

"So how did you get away?"

"When the shooting started, I eased in the house and me and Dijuana went out the back window."

"Well listen, T-Money is on the way over here because he has something to say to you."

"What's up?"

"It's best if we just wait on him. But in the meantime, you should get another room so your girl can chill why we talk."

"She's cool. She can just stay in the bathroom."

"That's not going to happen and trust me, it's better this way."

"Why, what's going on?" Knock, knock, knock.

"That's Money. Let him in."

"What's up, Money?"

"It ain't nothing, Young World."

"Well, what is it that you want to say to me?"

"First of all, calm the fuck down! Secondly, where is Dijuana?"

"She is..." Knock, knock, knock. "That's her now."

"Well, send her to get the other room."

"Oh hey, T- Money."

"What's up Dijuana?"

"Well, it's been kind of hectic tonight but considering the circumstances, we're alright. Right, baby?"

"Yeah, but listen, I need you to go downstairs and get another room."

"Okay, you want it on the same floor?"

"Yeah."

"Okay, I'll be back."

"No, you just stay there. I'm coming."

"Well she's gone now, so what's up?"

"First of all, I never trusted your girl." Strapp said.

"You think I didn't know that! Every time she speaks to you, you just kind of stare at her."

"Yeah but as you are about to learn, there's a good reason. Young World, we had your girl checked out! Yeah you're right. But listen she has a lot of baggage."

"Like what, she's too pretty?"

"Well to be honest, yes! She's way too pretty to be in Parkhill projects."

"Listen at him T-Money, and you say we should trust his feelings."

"Let me ask you this, Young World. Where is she from?"

"She says she's from Alabama."

"Does she have any kids?"

"No! And I don't appreciate y'all asking me all these questions like I don't know my girl! Shit, we've been kicking it for months and you don't think I would know the questions y'all are asking."

"Well, apparently not!"

"What are you talking about?"

"For starters, your girl is not from Alabama and she has a six year old daughter named Sondra Nelson."

"Yeah, your girl is from Miami, Florida, home of all the big ballers."

"What is that supposed to mean?"

"It means why would a dime piece move from a place where she knows she can get paid to come to Ocala, Florida to stay in the poorest projects in town. Oh and before I forget she was supposed to be the victim in two home invasions where the boyfriends were left dead! And word on the Miami streets is that the family of one of the boyfriends is looking for her which would explain why she's here in Ocala!"

"Now, you don't have to be the smartest person in the world to see that something is wrong with this picture. But if you need to be sure then investigate her, yourself because if she tried to set you up, then the bitch must die! But in the meantime, there's a wedding tomorrow and y'all need to be there, so handle your B.I. and we'll see you tomorrow."

After T-Money and Strapp left Young World had to take in everything that was said. He knew that without a doubt that if Strapp had her checked out then everything they was saying was true. "But why was Strapp so damn suspicious? Was he just like that or was he envious of me? And then T-Money always backed what Strapp thought, no questions asked. But now, who was Dijuana Nelson?" Why hadn't she told him about her child? Why did she say she was from Alabama when she was really from Miami? "But most importantly, did she try to have me knocked off!" The more he thought about it, the more it seemed that Strapp was right. Hell, if I was a dope boy I would get at her myself. And then being from the bottom looking like that she should have everything she ever dreamed of. But it's all good because if she was trying to have him killed, the bitch would have to die. And if not, then life will go on.

"Hey Black, while you were in the hospital, I heard on the radio that we killed those two fed fuck ups."

"Well, that's two less feds the dope boys have to worry about. But on a serious note, we need to find that nigga and my bitch ass cousin and finish that business!"

"What about your arm?"

"The doctor said the bullet went in and out, so it ain't nothing but some pain."

"And we both know if it ain't no pain, then there can be no gain!"

CHAPTER 17

St. John Baptist Church was filled to the capacity. Mrs. Hampton had outdone herself but she had no limits when it came to her beloved son.

"Ooh Mama, I'm so nervous." Sheena said.

"Just relax, baby and remember that mama loves you and the man you love will be right there with you."

"I mean it looks like the whole town is out there."

"Well, you have to remember that Terry is well liked throughout the city. As a word of advice, I will tell you to ignore the stress from some of the envious women in here. There are a lot of women who not only would die to be in your place but also a lot who have tried!"

"You're right, mama. I'm going to hold my head up high and smile all the way to the altar knowing that this is the first day of the rest of our lives."

"Well in that case, let's get ready to get that man."

"Ready when you are, Mrs. Hampton said as both women walked out the room.

"Well T-Money, this is it homie. Remember, no more late night booty calls. No more weekend booty calls. No more spoiling girls with lavish gifts and things like that!"

"To be honest homies, I haven't done those things in so long that it doesn't even cross my mind anymore. And besides all those things I can do to and with my wife."

"I wish you the best of luck with the married life and hope you enjoy it to the fullest."

"I really do appreciate that, Young World. It means a lot to me that y'all are here to share this day with me."

"Well, it's that time, playa, so let's make it happen!"

As the day unfolded, everything turned out beautiful. The wedding itself was like a fairytale but when T-Money came down the aisle singing "One in a Million" Sheena couldn't believe it as tears ran down her face at rapid speed. Mrs. Hampton was also in tears watching her son enjoy one of the best days of his life. You had to look real careful but even Strapp had tears in his eyes watching his main man get married. Strapp knew that the game was next! When a hustler like T-Money gets married, it's only natural to divorce the streets. He didn't know when but he knew it was coming and he would welcome it. The wedding really broke Young World up on the inside because he knew that this should have already happened to him. But to see his mentor get married made him just as happy.

Because Agents Marks and Brady was black, nobody even noticed the new faces in the crowd. After Agents Smith and Harris were killed, Marks and Brady was called in to investigate. Upon investigating both houses, they found notes on the investigation of Terry Hampton AKA T-Money, Toney Bean AKA Strapp and Jeremy Johnson AKA Young World. There were also notes saying that they had a confidential informant by the name of Dijuana Nelson. And all they had to do was find her! But little did they know her time in life would expire before they ever had a chance to meet her. They had hoped they would see her at the wedding but they didn't.

"Black, you think this is a good idea?"

"Hell yeah! We know he's gonna be at his main man's wedding so all we have to do is follow him to his house and handle our business."

"Hopefully, my bitch ass cousin is there too so we can kill two birds with one stone."

"Well Money, go ahead and enjoy yourself and me and Strapp will holla at you later."

"Okay, but when I get back next week, we gonna all sit down and talk alright."

"No problem, dawg. Just make sure you have a good time."

"Yeah, and don't do nothing I wouldn't do." Strapp said.

"Well, I guess that means everything goes."

"Ha, ha, ha, ha, ha, ha, ha, be easy homie."

"Hey Young World, don't forget about what we talked about earlier."

"Nah, I'm about to check that out right now and then I'll get back with you."

"Well alright, remember, I'm just a phone call away."

Young World had indeed put a lot of thought into what Money and Strapp had told him. It bothered him so bad that he had to put her through a test and she failed badly. He had called and told her to pack for a weekend getaway and they would leave as soon as he got there. When Young World arrived and told her they were going to Miami, she turned white in the face and came up with all type of excuses even though she was already packed. It had took Young World a little thought because of his feelings but he realized that she had to die! So he had already made up his mind to kill her when he came from the wedding. He tried to think of how he was going to do it while he was at the wedding she didn't want to go to. But after thinking about it, he decided she didn't deserve no better death than all the dudes he had killed and that's how it would go down.

When Young World pulled up in front of his house he didn't see Dijuana's car, so he jumped out and went inside the house unaware of his surroundings.

"Alright Carlos, he's in the house so let's make our move, get this cash and be out!"

"Dijuana, where are you at?" Young World shouted as he walked up the stairs. When he got in the room, he found a note on the bed.

Dear Jeremy,

My time with you has been beautiful. I never in a million years thought that I would find a guy like you. But I'm so sorry that we didn't meet under different circumstances where things could have been different. I will tell you this though, beware of Black and Carlos because they want what you have and they've already tried to take it once. And thank you for your love because if not for that I know I would have been dead last night. I know you know about me and my past and I know Strapp told you. If it's worth anything, you should always trust his instinct because he was suspicious of me from day one. Well, I hope we don't meet again because I know that would be bad for me. So keep your head and stay strong.

Love always,
Dijuana

On the hunt.

After reading the letter, Young World couldn't do nothing but smile. He was truly mad and would have killed her if she would have been there! But in a way his heart was glad she made it. Young World knew he had to deal with Black and Carlos, so he was on his way out but was surprised when he got down stairs.

"Well, well, well, if it isn't the famous Young World."

"What the fuck y'all niggas want?"

"Shut up, bitch ass nigga and tell us where that money is!"

"Ha, ha, ha, ha, ha."

"Oh, you think that's funny!"

"Hell yeah! Because if y'all knew anything about me, you would have known I was a true soldier."

"What the fuck is that supposed to mean?"

"It means kiss my ass and bury me a gangster." It was at that time, Young World went for his gun. Boom, boom, boom, boom, boom!

"Silly ass nigga! Should have just gave up the money. Let's search this bitch, Carlos and get the fuck up out of here."

"Did you hear that?"

"Yeah, those were gunshots. Call for backup, ASAP!"

"Gunshots fired. Officer requesting back up at 1822 S.W. 5th Place."

"10-4. Back up is on the way."

"Hey Black, you hear that?"

"Yeah, it sounds like them folks."

"Damn, that's fucked up!"

"Fuck it man, grab that jewelry and let's go." As Black and Carlos eased out the back door, the police were arriving at the scene.

"Agent Marks, what do you want us to do?"

"Surround the perimeter and make sure there's no escape. Let me see that bullhorn. Alright in the house, come out with your hands up! I'm gonna count to ten and then we're coming in to get you. This is your last warning! Okay, all teams green light, green light!" When the feds and police busted down the door and went in; they were surprised at what they found.

"Get an ambulance here, right now! Right now, got damn it!"

"Is he going to make it/"

"It's hard to call right now because he's lost a lot of blood."

"Well, do all you can because we need this one to live."

Ring, ring, ring. "Yeah, what's up?"

"Strapp, this is Diane down at the hospital. You need to come here right away because Young World has been shot!" The dial tone was all she heard because Strapp was out the door. When Strapp got to the hospital, he saw police and feds everywhere. He didn't even care to take his guns off him as he headed in the hospital to find out what happened to his friend.

"Excuse me sir, you can't go in there."

"The fuck I can't, that's my family in there!"

"I understand how you must feel but you can't go in because he's in surgery."

"Well, I ain't going nowhere until somebody tells me what happened!"

"Well one minute, sir."

"Excuse me, Agents Mark and Brady, there's a young man who seems very upset and says he ain't leaving until he finds out what's going on."

"Where is he now?"

"Standing by the door." When Agents Marks and Brady saw who was at the door they knew there would be hell to pay. Tony Bean AKA Strapp was rumored to be a cold blooded killer and known for keeping guns on him at all times.

"Excuse me, sir, how may we help you?"

"That's my family in there and I want to know what happened to him!"

"How do you know who that is sir?"

"Listen man, I don't have time for a game of 21 questions, so just tell me what I want to know or I can wait until the doctor comes out." Seeing the look on his face Agent Marks could tell that he was upset and he didn't want to add to the problems so he decided to tell. "Well it seems, someone shot Mr. Johnson six to eight times and he's lost a great deal of blood, so he's fighting for his life in surgery as we speak." There were no words needed to see the pain in Strapp's face as his eyes turned blood shot red and a single tear fell from his eye.

"Do you know who could have wanted to hurt Mr. Johnson?"

"No I don't but I will say this! If I find out before y'all do, there will be no need to worry about an investigation!"

"Excuse me, sir. Are you the immediate family of the patient?"

"Yes ma'am, I am."

"Well the good news is that he's alive and he's stable. But the bad news is that Mr. Johnson went into a coma about thirty minutes ago. I'm sorry sir, we did all we could."

"I know. Can I go in to see him?"

"Sure, go right ahead. Your voice may bring him back out of the coma."

"Before you go, Mr. Bean, we would like to ask you a few questions."

"Questions, Questions! Man, fuck a question! I told you everything I know already besides I wasn't there so how the hell could I help you?"

"Well if anything comes to mind, give us a call."

"Man, let's be real. I don't know shit and if I did, I wouldn't tell y'all shit anyway! I don't like the police, the feds or anybody else in a muthafuckin' suit, so leave me the fuck alone!"

As Strapp walked in Young World's room, he couldn't stop the tears that ran from his eyes and even if he could, there was no reason to. Young World had become family to him and it was killing him to see his family in this condition. "Damn Young World, what did you get into? Just stay strong and hold on because we need you out here with us. And don't worry about who did this to you because as soon as I find out, they're dead and that's a promise!" (As the agents watched Strapp leave the hospital they both knew one thing, somebody had hell to pay!)

CHAPTER 18

"Sheena, call and find out what time our flight leaves."

"I already did, boo and you have one hour before the plane leaves so hurry up and take your shower so we won't be late."

"Well, why don't you come help me out?"

"No because if I did that, we wouldn't make the flight."

"Ha, ha, ha, ha. At least you know me."

"Yeah, well I'll just watch T.V. until you get out."

Ring, ring, ring. "Hello."

"What's up, Sheena?"

"Strapp, is that you?"

"Yeah, it's me sis. Where is that husband of yours?"

"Oh, he's in the shower. You want me to tell him to call you before we leave?"

"No, this can't wait! I hate to spoil y'all honeymoon but this needs to come from me."

"Strapp, what happened?"

"Young World got shot and he's in a coma."

"Oh my God, no."

"Baby, who is that on the phone? Sheena, what's wrong?"

"Hello, who is this?"

"It's me, Money. Young World got shot and he's in a coma."

"We're on our way."

When T-Money and Sheena got to the hospital he wanted to talk to the doctor who performed the operation. "Excuse me; are you the doctor that operated on Jeremy Johnson?"

"No. That would be Doctor Brown."

"Well, is he in?"

"Just a minute and I'll get him for you."

"Yes sir, how may I help you?"

"My brother was shot and he's now in a coma, right?"

"That's correct."

"First thing I want to say that money is not the issue so as long as he's in a coma just monitor him and secondly, what are his chances of coming out of this?"

"You may be able to answer that better than me."

"And how is that Doctor?"

"Is he strong-minded?"

"Yes."

"Is he a fighter?"

"Yes."

"Does he have a reason to keep living?"

"Of course."

"Then I would say that his chances are pretty good."

"Thank you for your time Doctor."

"Don't mention it but do me one favor."

"What's that doc?"

"Try bringing someone or something close to him on a different level than yourself and he might come back quicker."

As T-Money and Sheena left the hospital, he could do nothing but think about what the doctor said. Besides him and Strapp there was no one else. "Baby, are you okay?"

"I was just thinking about what the doctor said and I can't think of anyone else.

"What about Uncle Sha?"

"That's his uncle true enough but me and Strapp are closer than him. And the only woman that he had love for is dead."

"So what are we gonna do, baby?"

"I don't know, Sheena. I just don't know."

"Agent Marks, did your intel pay off?"

"It sure did, Dijuana Nelson is now living in Orlando, Florida and is working at the Holiday Inn right off of Highway 75."

"Well what are we waiting on to pick her up when she is our only suspect in all this mess?"

"Oh, one of my buddies owes me a favor so she'll be picked up within the hour."

"That's good so we can start making a few arrests."

"How may I help you, today?"

"Well, we don't know Dijuana, why don't you tell us."

"Excuse me, sir. What are you talking about?" Dijuana tried to keep a straight face but her eyes betrayed her as well as the picture that they had of her.

"Ms. Nelson, you're under arrest. Anything you say can and will be used against you in a court of law. You have the right to an attorney. If you cannot afford one then the courts will provide one for you. Do you understand these rights?"

"Fuck you!"

"We are at the hotel, why not? Ha, ha, ha, ha, ha."

Meanwhile, back in the projects, Strapp was venting trying to cope with all that happened in just a matter of hours but in this case it would prove to be costly.

"Say dawg, you got that work?"

"Man, who the fuck are you?"

"My name is Twan. I used to deal with Young World but I haven't heard from him since I got back in town today." Now normally, Strapp would never deal hand-to-hand but he had so much on his mind that he abandoned all of his street senses.

"Well, what you trying to get playa?"

"Let me spend the same thing."

"Say playa, I'm not Young World, remember."

"Oh my bad, dawg. Let me get a half bird."

"Wait a minute." Strapp went into the empty house across the projects and came back with a brown paper bag. "Here you go playa. Now where is that 12 piece?"

"Twelve! I thought it was ten."

"Like I told you before, I'm not Young World so if you can't handle it then let me know."

"Don't panic dawg, I got you. Here you go. Oh and tell Young World to get at me." As soon as Strapp made the sale all his street smarts came back to him, only it was too late! The sale had been made and all he could hope was that it didn't cost him.

"Well, well, well. Ms. Nelson, we've been looking for you. After all, you did leave town pretty quick after Agents Smith and Harris died."

"Am I supposed to know them?"

"Look Ms. Nelson, cut the bullshit! We already know that you are the informant that they had on this case. Now if you don't want to talk to us then I guess we need to charge you with these conspiracy and murder charges. And you will have all of your life to figure out why you wouldn't help yourself."

"Okay, okay. What do you want to know?"

"Hold on, let me get paper and pen. Now start from the beginning and don't leave nothing out."

After two hours of interrogation, the feds learned more information than they could have if they would have been deep cover. She told them that Terry Hampton AKA T-Money was the brains of the operation and that he would give Jeremy Johnson AKA Young World and Tony Bean AKA Strapp anywhere from 50 to 100 kilos of cocaine to distribute throughout the city. This was really enough to make the arrest but to get the conspiracy that they wanted they would need one of the three to slip up and make a sell to one of their informants. With Jeremy in a coma and Strapp being the most unlikely to slip, their chances were slim.

"Are Agents Marks or Brady in?"

"Who may I say wants to know."

"I'm one of their street informants."

"Well, just have a seat and one of them will be right with you."

"Excuse me Agent Marks, but one of your street informants is here and says he needs to see you."

"Gentlemen, excuse me while I see to this matter."

"Okay, we'll wait until you come back to see what our next move will be."

"Twan, what's so important that you had to come down to the station?"

"Well sir, I thought you would like to know that I just made a buy of 18 ounces."

"That's a good bust but I'm in a very important meeting."

"I understand sir, but maybe you want to know who made the sale."

"Well, who was it/"

"None other than Strapp!"

"Strapp, as in Tony Bean!"

"That's the one sir and it's all on tape."

"Come on back son and let's get you that money."

"Money, do you think that this will work?"

"I don't know Strapp but I was reading in a book that sometimes talking can bring someone out of a coma. And if talking can bring them back then a good nut should surely snap him out of it."

"Hell right now, I'm just trying to get our nigga back and if some head will do it then I'm all for it. So Sunshine, you think you still got it?"

"Hell yeah! If I can't bring him back then I might retire." Sunshine was a stripper that T-Money and Strapp ran into after a party one night and as advertised the head was off the chain! So T-Money figured that if anybody could wake him up, Sunshine was definitely the one.

"Well gentlemen, this is it. Tomorrow the judge will sign off on the indictment and we'll be able to arrest both T-Money and Strapp. And when and if Mr. Johnson ever comes out of his coma, he too will be arrested."

"Do we have enough to get a conviction?"

"With Ms. Nelson and my informant, there's no way we can lose."

"Alright Strapp, you hold the door down and don't let anybody in. Alright Sunshine, do what you do!"

"Damn! This little fella is packing a pretty nice load."

"Spare us the details and get busy." After four or five minutes of what seemed to be the toe curling head, Young World just laid flat still.

"Damn Sunshine, you couldn't do nothing for our boy but I'll be damned if I let you get away tonight without getting me some." Strapp said.

"Shit Strapp, if I hadn't got married, I would have to have some too. Ha, ha, ha, ha, ha."

"Well, why don't you just consider it a wedding gift?"

"Now that doesn't sound like a bad idea."

Ring, ring, ring. "Yeah, what's up?"

"Hey baby, listen up and listen real good. The feds are going to arrest you and T-Money tomorrow on some indictments."

"What!"

"The way I hear it some girl named Dijuana Nelson is supposed to testify on Young World and y'all."

"That is a problem but they need more than that."

"Well apparently, you sold some guy name Twan half of the house if you know what I mean. And it turns out that he is one of the feds' informants."

"Damn!"

"What's up, Strapp?"

"Hold on. You sure it's tomorrow?"

"Yes, because the judge can't sign off on it until then."

"Okay boo, good looking and I'll holla at you."

"Alright, but keep your phone on you so if I hear something else I can call you."

"Alright, peace out."

"Talk to me, Strapp. What's going on?"

"Money, I fucked up! You know that was my connect down at the station and she says the feds are indicting us tomorrow."

"On what charges?"

"Conspiracy with intent and sells to a federal informant."

"But what sales?"

"Today, I was so upset I wasn't thinking and sold to this dude Twan a half a bird."

"Is that all they have?"

"Nah, they got the bitch Young World was messing with in the projects to testify also."

"Well listen, I figured this could happen one day with our lifestyle so it shouldn't surprise you that I have a plan. But let's drop Sunshine back off and I will tell you then."

"Well, does anybody plan on telling me?" In one motion, everybody turned around to see a wide awake Young World. Both T-Money and Strapp rushed to his bed. Together they all embraced and once again the tears of the gangsters were exposed.

CHAPTER 19

After the doctors came and checked on Young World and made sure he was alright, the guys sent Sunshine in a cab to get a room and wait on one of them to arrive.

"Alright fellas, this is the plan. We are going to jail but the case will be dismissed."

"How is that?"

"Because both of their key witnesses will be dead."

"Man, you know if that happens we will be the number one suspects."

"I know. That's why we gonna turn ourselves in tomorrow. That will be our alibi. All I need for you to do is to get Twan's address from your connect at the station and everything else will fall into place."

"Man, you sure we shouldn't just leave the country?"

"For what and be running our whole life! Trust me Strapp; I don't want to go to prison neither but this is the best way."

Alright then, let's make it happen."

"But first, let's go holla at Sunshine just in case!"

At 11:00 a.m. the next day, T-Money, Strapp and Young World were getting ready to turn themselves in. Strapp's connect had just called and told them that the judge signed the indictment based on the government's two key witnesses. "Alright fellas, let's do this shit so we can get back on the streets."

"We just gonna walk right in and turn ourselves in?"

"Yep."

"Well, won't they be suspicious?"

"It doesn't matter because we have the element of surprise on our side."

"Alright officers, approach with caution as these fellas are considered armed and dangerous."

"Excuse me; we need to turn ourselves in." When the agents turned around and saw all three of them, T-Money, Strapp and Young World, the whole precinct got quiet.

"There is a warrant for our arrest, isn't there?"

"Well, well, well. What a surprise? To what do we owe the pleasure of y'all turning yourselves in?"

"Are you gonna talk us to death or take us to our cell."

"Right this way, big mouth!" When the three of these guys turned their selves in, the agents were lost. Here they all were facing ten years to life on conspiracy charges and they just walk in and turned themselves in. Agent Marks and Brady just considered it a blessing because they knew with the two key witnesses that they had it was gonna be impossible to beat the charges. So anyway it went they were happy it was over.

Several months passed by waiting what was supposed to be a major blow to the drug rings that were in Marion County. Terry Hampton AKA T-Money, Tony Bean AKA Strapp and Jeremy Johnson AKA Young World, who the feds labeled Triple Threat, were three of Marion County's most feared drug dealers. But today would be the beginning of the end as the government decided to rush to the point of their two key witnesses. The way the government saw it was, the quicker they could get this over the better.

"Well Money, I hope this works." Young World said. "Because if not we're going down for a long time."

"Yeah, you're right Young World, but I think we will have the last laugh!"

"The way I see," Strapp said, "we had a good run in the game if this is the end. And besides that bitch Sunshine sucked and fucked a nigga so good I could do 5 to 10 just off of that! Ha, ha, ha, ha, ha!"

"Yeah, that bitch was off the chain last night! Hell I couldn't even make love to the wifey because she had sucked all the energy out of me. I should have known better because anytime a bitch can bring a nigga out of a coma by sucking his dick then the bitch ain't nothing to be played with! Ha, ha, ha, ha, ha."

"Hell, I'm glad y'all found that vacuum cleaner mouth ass ho! If not I might still be in a fucking coma!"

"You better believe one thing my nigga! If we had to go all over the world, we would have gotten you out of that coma."

"And that's real Young World because we all we got and that's more than most people will ever have."

"I love y'all niggas too."

"Ah shit nigga, don't go getting all soft on us now nigga. Especially since we might be going to prison! Ha, ha, ha, ha, ha,"

"Well let's hope that T-Money knows his shit and then we won't have to worry about that."

"Hampton, Johnson and Bean, let's go."

"Okay fellas, here we go!"

When they got in the courtroom, it was if the Super Bowl was in town. The courtroom was so packed that it was standing room only. "Order! Order in this courtroom or I'll have all of you held in contempt of court and this will be a private case hearing." When the judge said private, the whole courtroom fell silent. No one wanted to miss this so there was nothing to be said.

"Everybody stand! The Honorable Judge William T. Smith is now here. Bailiff, what do we have?"

"The United States vs. Terry Hampton, Toney Bean and Jeremy Johnson."

"What are the charges?"

"Conspiracy with the intent to distribute more than 100 grams."

"Good morning to both counsels."

"Good morning, your Honor."

"Court is now in session. Prosecution, call your witness."

"The prosecution calls Dijuana Nelson to the stand!"

"Ms. Nelson, how do you know the defendants?"

"I was the girlfriend of Jeremy Johnson for some months."

"What about Mr. Hampton and Mr. Bean?"

"They are friends of Jeremy."

"Is it true that these three run a cocaine operation?"

"Yes sir, it is."

"And how do you know this?"

"Well on several occasions, I was with Jeremy when he picked up his drugs from both T-Money and Strapp."

"When you say T-Money and Strapp, who are you referring to?"

"Mr. Hampton and Mr. Bean."

"So you have seen drugs and money exchange hands between all three of them?"

"Yes sir, I have."

"No more questions, your Honor."

"Counsel, would you like to cross examine?"

"Not at this time. Your Honor, it has just been bought to my attention that some important evidence we need will not be here until tomorrow so I ask the court for a recess until that time."

"Prosecution, do you have a problem with that?" Now being that the prosecution was so sure of their case, the lead attorney had no problem with it.

"No sir, your Honor, we do not."

"Okay, this court is adjourned until 9:00 a.m. tomorrow morning."

Now when Dijuana heard this she instantly grew worried. "Excuse me prosecutor, what is going on?"

"Oh don't worry; it's just a stall tactic by the defense. Just go back to your hotel and come back in the morning."

"Okay, but is there anything to worry about?"

"No, trust me. It will be over before you know it."

"Well okay, I'll see you in the morning."

"Oh one more thing, Mr. Parker will be riding back to the room with you so he can testify tomorrow also."

"That's fine with me. I could use the company."

On the way to the hotel, Dijuana and Twan were so busy getting to know each other that they didn't notice the lady cab driver had passed the hotel room until they were headed out of town.

"Hey excuse me, where are you going?" The driver said nothing.

"Ms., I'm sorry but you missed the exit to the hotel." Still the driver said nothing.

"Twan, say something to her!"

"Stop the got damn car bitch and let us out!" Finally the driver speaks.

"Now that's no way to talk to the wife of the infamous T-Money! Yes, wife. Oops, maybe I shouldn't have said that but since y'all never live to tell it, I thought I would share that with you. Ha, ha, ha, ha, ha!"

Sheena then drove to an empty field where she poured gas all over the car.

"Well, is there anything you want me to tell the judge?"

(352)

"Please, please, don't do this. We'll leave town and won't ever come back. Just please let us go."

"You should have thought about that before you decided to be a snitch! How about you sir, do you have anything to say?"

"Fuck you, bitch!"

"Now that's what I like, a man with big balls. But in any case, it's too late to try and be a real man now so, goodbye." Sheena lit a match and tossed it on the car and then got into her car and drove off smiling.

Meanwhile, back at the jailhouse T-Money, Strapp and Young World were watching the news. 'We interrupt the news broadcast to bring you a breaking news cast. Just minutes ago, a taxi cab was burned to a crisp with what seems to be two dead bodies inside. Police on the scene say that the bodies have yet to be identified but do know that it's a man and a woman. And that's our breaking new on News Center 12.'

"Damn, that's fucked up!" Strapp said.

"What's that?"

"Man did you hear what they said?"

"Yeah, they said a man and a woman got burned to death in a taxi cab."

"Well, don't you think that's fucked up?"

"That depends on who the passengers were."

"Man, that's still fucked up!"

"Well, that's them. Let's just get some rest for tomorrow."

"Yeah, I sure hope that your lawyer knows what he's doing."

"Y'all just chill. We will be okay, trust me!"

"Hampton, you have a visitor. Let's go."

"I'll be back, fellas. Y'all hold it down."

"Alright. If that's Mrs. Hampton tell her we said hello."

"Alright."

When T-Money stepped into the visitation room all he could see was a smiling Sheena.

"Baby, did you catch the news?"

"Yes I did, baby!"

"Did you hear about those poor people in the taxi cab?"

"Yeah, that's just awful isn't it?"

"Yeah but maybe it was they're time to go."

"Maybe it wasn't but I'll see you in court in the morning."

"Okay baby, I love you."

"I love you, too!"

The next morning at the police station, things were just about to get hectic. Ring, ring, ring. "Hello. Ocala Police Department, how may I direct your call?"

"Agents Marks or Brady, please."

"Who may I say is calling?"

"This is Dan, down at the morgue."

"One minute please."

"Agent Marks, Dan from the morgue is on line two."

"Okay, thank you Pamela."

"Hello. Agent Marks here."

"Agent Marks, this is Dan from the morgue and I thought you might like to know the identity of those bodies that were found in that cab."

"Who was it?"

"The lady was Dijuana Nelson and the man was Twan Parker."

"What! Is this some kind of joke?"

"No sir it isn't but I've been following the trial so I know you needed to know."

"Well alright, thanks for nothing!"

"Who was that, Agent marks?"

"You don't want to know. You just don't want to know."

"Okay, court is in session. Your Honorable Judge William T. Smith is here."

"Counsel, are you ready to continue?"

"Yes sir, we are your Honor."

"Your Honor, the prosecution wishes to approach the bench."

"Come forward."

"It has been bought to our attention that both of our key witnesses were killed in a car accident yesterday."

"I'm sorry to hear that."

"I'm sorry to hear it too, your Honor but if the prosecution does not have any witnesses then I have to ask that the charges against my clients be dismissed."

"Prosecution, do you have an objection?"

"No sir, your Honor, because without those witnesses we have no case."

"Well, then I guess that's it then. Take your spots."

"At this time, the courts have dismissed all charges against Mr. Hampton, Mr. Bean and Mr. Johnson. Court is adjourned." At the sound of the ruling, the courtroom went crazy. Mrs. Hampton almost fainted with joy as her son was now a free man. Sheena, too, went crazy as he jumped up and down hugging all three of the guys.

"Damn," Strapp and Young World said. "I wonder what happened."

"I told you yesterday that it depended on who was in that cab."

"Hell, well I guess it wasn't so fucked up then!"

"No it wasn't. Now if y'all don't mind, I have a honeymoon to start."

As T-Money and all of his family and friends left, Agents Marks and Brady just sat and watched.

"I'll get them Agent Brady. I'll get them if it's the last thing I do!"

The End

ABOUT THE AUTHOR

Author Terrant(hop) Hamilton is a Ocala, FL native whose roots run deep in the community. Son of a beautiful mother (Queen Hamilton) and a proud father of four (Terry, Daquan, Taysia and Jordan). A former drug dealer turned author & business owner (Ms Queens Thrift shop). His truth is a testament (All Things Are Possible With God) that the doors that God open, man can't close!

Last of a dying breed!

Checkmate!

Printed in the United States
By Bookmasters